Let Me Tell You Another Story,
a
"DIRTY DOZEN"
and
"WAG A TALE"

Charles Keith Hardman

ARCHWAY
PUBLISHING

This is a work of fiction. All of the characters, names, incidents, organizations, and dialogue in this novel are either the products of the author's imagination or are used fictitiously.

Archway Publishing books may be ordered through booksellers or by contacting:

Archway Publishing
1663 Liberty Drive
Bloomington, IN 47403
www.archwaypublishing.com
1 (888) 242-5904

ISBN: 978-1-4808-5167-2 (sc)
ISBN: 978-1-4808-5168-9 (e)

Library of Congress Control Number: 2017953207

Print information available on the last page.

Archway Publishing rev. date: 09/27/2017

Contents

Introduction

People always want to hear a good story. Sometimes these stories scare them though. That is where I come in. I make up stories and tales that people wouldn't think could ever be told. I write about things that go bump in the night and can only be seen in nightmares or by using a person's imagination to see the world differently. I like to scare people or to make them laugh when and if they read me. This collection of writings is not for the timid. It will take you to places that you never could dream of. Sex is not counted out! "Let me tell you another story" and "Wag a tale." I am sure that you haven't heard this one before? If I was in the sixties I would say that you are about to enter the Twilight Zone! But in the two thousands, I am saying, WINK! "Let me tell you another story" and "Wag a tale." Get ready for the next generation of short writings. There are no boundaries! Just be sure you can wink? I can. Now read "Let me tell you another story" and "Wag a tale." Two books turned into one.

Book One

"LET ME TELL YOU ANOTHER STORY"

Writer note:

Most people when they think of witches in America think about the white witches of Salem Massachusetts, but in fact witches in America come in all sorts of size, shape, color, religions, races, and powers. Some worship the Devil, others are from pagan lore and some come from the islands. Some Africans believe that witches are both male and female and in Europe witches and warlocks were believed to meet in the forests to do who knows what. Then there are the voodoo witches. They are believed to be able to bring back the dead or haunt a person anywhere in the world with their voodoo dolls. This is one such story about one of these voodoo witches. Be careful on your next island trip or visit to New Orleans. There are coffee colored witches that practice voodoo. Life is strange. If you live among the bayous and swamps of Louisiana and Texas then you might just come across people that will tell you tales of witchcraft and voodoo. Some believe them to be true and others want to capture them. Just beware if you want to capture one. It might just be more voodoo than you can handle. This is just one such story. "I shiver."

SMOKE ON THE BAYOU

RANSOM

RANSOM AWOKE IN A BED with his hands and legs tied with hemp rope so that he was unable to move much. He smelled incense or many herbs burning near him. The room had a hazy smoky atmosphere that was making his head spin. He wasn't sure what was happening to him after meeting Patricia on Bourbon Street two days before Mardi Gras. She confessed to him that she was a voodoo witch. He cared less! She brought him to her cabin on a bayou. He awoke tied to a bed. He wasn't surprised. In fact he was happy. He noticed a white powder surrounding the bed in what seemed like a circle to him. He guessed that it was night. He was pretty sure that he was in a nightmare of some sort but was not so sure he didn't want to be in this one. He was a willing sacrifice to whatever Patricia had in store for him. He wanted to be her voodoo man. Ransom wanted into Patricia's world. If he had to go in as a sacrificial goat, then so be it. He remembered nothing after she blew a powder in his face after he told her he didn't care that she was a voodoo witch. Now he was tied to a bed in hemp ropes and Patricia was going to control the rest of his life.

Patricia stood at the foot of the bed just staring at Ransom. She then spoke words that Ransom couldn't understand. He raised his head and screamed at Patricia,

"I want to be your voodoo man!"

Dr John's "Creole Moon" was playing in the background. Ransom wasn't sure that he was on earth, much less in New Orleans. He smelled shrimp boiling and lots of spices cooking in a nearby kitchen. A dog began barking. He had to be somewhere near a bayou. He knows he is still alive and must be under the influence of some sort of drug. Patricia leans over the foot of the bed and laughs loud and wet and then speaks in english.

"I will make you a voodoo man, but beware of what you ask for?"

She speaks these words with an accent that must have come from living on an island in the Caribbean.

Ransom's head is still foggy but he manages to squeal out a response.

"I will give you anything that you want."

"Becoming a voodoo man is not going to be that easy. You will have to go through some physical changes and your mind will fight with your body. Are you ready to become a voodoo man?"

Ransom was tied by his hands and feet with hemp rope which were strong and rough and were chaffing his wrists and ankles. He knows that if he struggles he will have some serious rope burns. He smells the strong odors coming from the burning incense or herbs and he can tell he is drifting into a trance of some sort. He speaks while he can.

"I will become whatever you want me to become. I will even sell my soul to the Devil if that is what you ask."

He was still under Patricia's spell. He could still smell the powder she blew into his face earlier.

Patricia let out a squeal, then tickles his foot with an owl's feather. She strips him naked and mounts him. She makes him shoot his juices into her. She lets her body absorb all of him. She will drain his soul from him. He wants to give her his soul. Now she will accept it. She is a voodoo witch that is taking a soul.

Patricia thinks she is a powerful voodoo witch. Ransom is now going to be treated like a dog because she wants power. He will give up his soul to a new voodoo witch. She is not a scary witch though and has been looking for a strong soul to capture to gain powers. Ransom seems to have one. She just doesn't know what to do with it. She decides to test his soul and throws more herbs on the fire. Ransom screams because he is a soul under Patricia's spell. He wants to give her his soul and she is willing to accept it. She lets his fluids drip from her pussy. She walks toward her kitchen and finishes absorbing most of his soul. She is now going to become a powerful voodoo witch that controls a human's soul. She never thought that she could control such a human soul. She really doesn't know what to do next. She feels the power though and is forced to shout out loud.

"I am not of this earth. I am now two people."

She mounts Ransom again and drains more of his juices. She wants to suck him dry this time. Patricia now feels that she owns Ransom's soul. She feels his life-force enter her body. Ransom will now enter this world as a empty corpse. Patricia will own his and her souls. She looks down at Ransom's corpse. It looks dried up and shriveled. It will never breathe or struggle in life again. It is just a corpse. It even has a smile on it's dead face. Ransom has given her his soul. She just created her first zombie.

Patricia stands and looks out at the bayou. It is just a water source trying to find it's way to the ocean to her. It will eventually get there but it will not be an easy journey. Ransom and many others have given their souls to voodoo witches in the past. Patricia just captured her first zombie. Patricia is now a voodoo witch attached to a human soul. She now feels the life sources of two souls inside her. She unties the hemp ropes that hold Ransom to the bed. She looks down at Ransom's corpse and makes it rise.

"You will now do my bidding. You are now a corpse that walks on this earth without a soul You will become my first zombie."

She laughs aloud. She really feels like a powerful voodoo witch. Patricia wants to become the Queen of voodoo witches in New Orleans. She is just a baby though, as she just took control of her first zombie. She again laughs loud and hard. She knows she will need a lot more zombies before she can become the Queen of the voodoo witches. Ransom is a good start though as his soul is very powerful.

Patricia turns and again stares out at the bayou when Ransom, now a zombie, comes up behind her and sticks a large knife in her back and forces it upwards into her heart. He never got to tell her that his mother was also a voodoo witch and she was experienced in controlling zombies. Patricia died before she had a chance to learn how to control a zombie. Witches must know their competition if they are to continue. Ransom was sent by his mother to kill her competition. "Witches?

The queens have children.

Writer note:

What if you had two of the most unpopular wars in United States history happen approximately 100 years apart with two of the most dynamic presidents running the country and both of them being assassinated and replaced by a person with the last name Johnson? These wars would also produce some of the most damaged of all soldiers ever made to try and return to a normal life in the United States. PTSD is now a regular part of a soldier's treatment when he comes home from a war. Viet Nam and the Civil War produced too many soldiers not able to enter back into the world they left before becoming a soldier. These wars were not wars that were going to be won easily and all that fought in them in America and Asia would have to deal with coming home to a place that had forsaken them. There is no answer to give to these soldiers. Either they were against it and forced to fight it or they volunteered to avoid prison or to make their parents happy. There was just no way for them to come home without being damaged goods. Here is a sad, sad story. I cry every day when I see a street person that was a casualty of the Viet Nam War. It was a bad war. Here is a story that makes me weep at night. Two wars that no one won! We then and now have to deal with the wounded.

UNKNOWN SOLDIERS

I NEVER ENLISTED INTO THE army during the Viet Nam War. I just went to college. What I saw come back from Viet Nam were not soldiers but damaged goods. I couldn't buy into what was being sold as reality back then because I lived with Viet Nam veterans that cut the ears off of people. They wore neaklaces with ears they cut off the enemy. They came back damaged and often broken. They were drug addicts or worse. They thought they would become soldiers but they were turned into killers. They were asked to kill and then forget that they had done so. This was not so easily forgotten for a great many of them. They wanted to become soldiers but they ended up damaged goods. They could never forget what they were asked to do. They were mercenaries that returned to America and were asked to forget the Hell that they had to live with. Killing was in their blood. They killed people and were now asked to forget about it. Could you? I don't think they could either. We now have to live with them. I call them the "UNKNOWN SOLDIERS." They have no way out. They went into a war that could never be won and became killers. They returned home with the smell of death on their hands. They killed people that they didn't know. They were now asked to live with people that ate at McDonalds everyday. They were not able to forget the smell of death. Their wives and children looked at them as heroes or veterans. They looked at each other as killers. They tasted the blood of killing someone. Think about it. If you killed, no matter the reason, and now you must try to enter a world that is wax papered into believing that the world you just exited doesn't exist. What vision would you see when you entered a house in a neighborhood that wasn't filled with people with guns and bombs trying to kill you? Death is just something their families were watching on the news. They never had to actually kill someone. These returning soldiers killed and now they needed to understand why? Some cut the ears off of their victims! They made necklaces out of their victims ears! Think about it? My next Macdonald burger could be part of a Vietcong! Some of them puke every morning thinking about how many bullets they have left in their rifle clip! They had to kill or die!

These people signed up to become a soldier or were drafted. Now they were returning as a person that needed an answer.

"Excuse me! I had to kill or be killed!"

This is not what a soldier needed to hear. Now they were coming home to a nation that admitted it lost the war. They were losers!

How could they join a community that had never killed a person?

War is never a good thing. Life in America has its bad points and sometimes the country has to send their sons and daughters to war, but now those children have come home.

What they do next is not for beginners. They have to make sense of what they had to see and do. They killed people and this is a fact. Death is real to them. America is living a in globe that needs to be shaken. Death is real in the world and these soldiers are trying to leave it behind. People die daily there and not always so easily. Sometimes they struggle to survive. Warriors are made and they don't always wake up with a good dream. Sometimes they wake up screaming.

Unknown soldiers are now everywhere. I woke up with one yesterday. She awoke screaming. I still don't know what was scaring her. She was not in my bed. She was in a forest somewhere far away. I held her tightly and made her feel calm. She still screamed so loud that I had to grip onto her like she needed to know that she was not going to die.

She held on to me like I was her life force. I now have a woman that I can love. She needs to know that there is a safe place. She came back damaged. Killers are now becoming a part of this world and they need to know there is someone here to just hold them until the terror subsides.

PTSD

Now this disease or mental illness has been around for centuries, maybe even thousands of years. I think maybe the Viet Nam War made it become a national problem though in the United States. The Civil war probably created the most cases of PTSD but because doctors just cut off limbs and hacked up bodies filled with lead bullets or that were shredded by cannon balls no one put a name to what the soldiers had to face. The Civil War in the 1860's was probably one of the most traumatic wars ever fought on this planet. If you were a modern psychiatrist that went to a battlefield after some sort of truce or whatever allowed each side to go among the dead and wounded and try to save a few of them, then you would probably vomit and run away. PTSD wasn't even thought of as a mental illness problem or something that could be treated back then. But brother against brother, a black living as someone's property was an everyday happening then. In fact a whole country was torn apart by hatred and greed. A slave was someone's property. It was accepted by the southern states since their beginnings. Was it legal? That was just up to who was in control. Now did slaves suffer from PTSD? Did the slave owners suffer from it? Did the abolitionists suffer from it? This is the problem. They fought an entire war in the United States for the first time. I guess you can say the genocide of the American Indian might be the first war totally fought on US soil, but then American Indians had even fewer rights than a slave in the southern states and they were slaughtered even more after the Civil War. So they were never really defeated and war was never really declared against them. They were just somewhere that the government wanted to populate their lands with someone else. But the states that had to regroup after the Civil War were filled with damaged people. Many soldiers lost limbs and had to figure out how to scratch out a living as a handicapped person. Other soldiers witnessed prisoner camps that could only be described as hellholes. Now some of the soldiers formed their own little outlaw groups and terrorized what was becoming cities in the midwest and south. Carpetbaggers came from the north. The soldiers that fought the Civil War became the first unknown soldiers. They had been forgotten and neither side really won. They just lived with the horror that was the Civil War and no one was going to come to their rescue. They were the unknown now because they had nowhere to turn to and no one wanted to look them in the eye or try to give them a helping hand. They were the first US soldiers to be swept under the carpet as PTSD. The problem was there was no US government that would admit that they had created this sickness among it's warriors. Most that fought in the Civil War would become the slaves that the war was supposed to free or worse. The Civil War created more damaged soldiers than any war in our history. The Viet Nam war though opened up some sores that still existed from the Civil War. Soldiers came home to see an army of students and middle class Americans that didn't respect them for fighting an unpopular war that was lost. They were now "Unknown Soldiers." History rose it's ugly head once again. PTSD became something that people could use to describe the damaged goods coming home from the most unpopular war in America's modern history. The soldiers were the victims. It really didn't matter what horrors they had lived through. They now had to adapt to a world that just wanted to forget. They were now just another rebel or yank that was laying in a field in Gettysburg, Shiloe, or Bull Run wondering why they were asked to risk their life and then be discarded as if they didn't matter. It was as if they had never been born. They had become unknown soldiers by just doing what their government told them to do. Now going to Nam was something they were told to do. Coming home was something they would need to understand. Being an unknown soldier is something that will make most soldiers a little, if not a lot crazy. PTSD can't answer the questions that are floating around in their heads. My girlfriend just practically raped me. She wants to forget. She is an unknown soldier. I hug her to let her know she is back in America.

DRAFTEES, CRIMINALS, AND THE REST

Lonnie Wilson is laying in tall grass. He has a wound to his shoulder. He grips his weapon with both hands. He is sure he will need it if he is going to survive this day. He bites his tongue and then yells as loud as he can. "Let's kill these mother fuckers." He stands and fires his rifle. He is on his last clip. There are only so many bullets that he can shoot and he is now at the end of his killing power. He looks out at a jungle filled with the enemy he was sent to kill. He only has one clip of bullets in his rifle left though. He will probably never see American soil again. He was drafted. He didn't volunteer. He was scared shitless. If he lived what would he tell his children and grand children?

Peter York was also drafted into the army. He had no military training or for that matter much other training in his life. He usually drank beer and played video games with his buddies. He received a notice in the mail that he was to report for induction into the army. He was eighteen years old. He couldn't even vote yet and now he was being asked to join the army. He went to the induction center and became a soldier. He was now a unknown soldier. He didn't volunteer for this. He was drafted into the army and now he was just trying to stay alive. As he stood emptying his rifle he wondered why he was there?

Paul Thompson was allowed to stay out of prison by joining the army and sent to Viet Nam. He robbed people for a living. He was good at it until he got caught. Now it was either prison or the army. Paul didn't like the idea of living behind bars. He chose the jungles of Viet Nam. He was not a soldier yet. He would become an unknown soldier though. The jungle has a way of making a man turn inside out. Paul was given a gun and told to survive. He just didn't fit in among soldiers. He was a criminal that thought he was owed a meal ticket. Paul was now in over his head. Viet Nam was his wake up call. He was now facing enemy fire and he would have to use his rifle as a weapon instead of just a meal ticket.

Brent Mason was born into a wealthy family. His father was a retired general in the Air Force. He enlisted in the Air Force to please his father. He was now a machine gunner on a helicopter. He just wasn't prepared to be this person. He was supposed to shoot at anything that moved. He kept his finger on the trigger. The life of a machine gunner in Viet Nam was less than six months. He was only on week two. He kept his finger on the trigger. He was now an unknown soldier.

Sally was a nurse and she thought she would be stationed in Saigon. It wasn't in her future. She was sent to Laos. It wasn't even Viet Nam but it didn't matter. Soldiers were dying there and needed medical care. She was flown in by helicopter and put on the front line. She was being asked to save soldiers that were under fire. She was given a M-16 and told how to pull the trigger. She wasn't trained to shoot weapons and now she was a unknown soldier. What happened to her there is still haunting her. She is now my girlfriend and is hugging me screaming. I want her back home, but I am not sure how to bring her back.

THE ENDING

So these people if they find a way to survive will have to come back to a America that has no idea what they had asked these people to do for their country. Most were ignorant and some were just stupid. Some thought they were joining in a family tradition. When they came back they would be damaged goods. They would never be the same person that signed up to fight an unpopular war. Now they would have to try and fit into a world that had no idea of the horror that they were sent into. They were "Unknown Soldiers." They had no idea what they were going to have to face in their future. Now they were coming home from a war that for all purposes was a lost war. We left too many people to die horrible deaths because they didn't have our weapons. I am not sure that most of the returning soldiers did not feel good about their tour of duty there. I know my girlfriend still has nightmares and hugs me like she is still back there.

I just thought people should understand that the returning soldiers from Viet Nam should be classified as "Unknown Soldiers." It was the second war that produced so many damaged American soldiers. May we never produce anymore of them. War makes people crazy! Now crazy has to come home! What will we do with the "Unknown Soldiers?"

No more useless wars has to be the answer. I am just not sure that this is possible! Wake up!

"UNKNOWN SOLDIERS?"

Writer's note.

This story is an introduction into another world. It is about a man who has killed and has remorse. He lines up seven guns on a table in front of him. He has used all but one of them in his profession. He kills people for a living. He is saving the seventh gun for his final act on this planet. His death. He doesn't know that the final gun was given to him by a witch. He is about to find out about the seventh gun and it's bullet and the witch.

second writer's note:

This story is very disturbing because it deals with life after death. What if you awoke on a stainless steel table in a morgue and you didn't know why? The only answer to the questions flowing through your mind should be why am I wearing a toe tag if I am still alive? A very disturbing story but a good read. Just trust me! This is a story that will keep your toe tapping!

TOE TAG

Lawrence awakes on a stainless steel table. He remembers shooting a bullet into his brain. He should be dead. He isn't though. The table is cold and he shivers. His mind is now awake and he is wondering why he is still alive? He is sure there will be other people thinking the same. He shot himself with a bullet in a gun that he was given in a coffee shop by a woman he could only remember as if she was just a blur. He just didn't know the seventh gun and single bullet was not for him to kill himself with. He now needs to find out why he is still alive! He removes the toe tag from his foot and stands up in the morgue. He is nude. He needs to find some clothes and a reason why he is not dead. He rummages through the lockers and finds sealed evidence clothing in sealed bags. He tears them open until he finds some clothing that make him look more than a homeless person. The clothes stink of death. He walks toward a door that will lead him out of the morgue. He wasn't autopsied so he was still a whole person. He finds the door that will lead him out of the morgue. He is living a nightmare. He smells like he hasn't bathed in days and he runs into the night as if he was knowing where he was going. He stops in the middle of a road and has to jump to the curb before being run over. He doesn't even know where he is. He grabs his head to try to remember the last thing he saw before pulling the trigger on the gun that was supposed to kill him. All he can see is empty pages. He just wanted to end his life. He rubs his eyes. He is all alone and has no memory. He is also wearing dead people's clothing and has no money. He is pretty much screwed and up the river without a paddle. He sits down on the curb and smiles. He looks at his feet. He is wearing one black sneaker and a white one. He laughs out loud. He used to be a killer is all he can recollect. He now remembers that the seventh gun and it's bullet were a gift. The person that gave it to him was a person that he only met once. He remembered that she looked like she was in a fog. He remembered watching her leave and turn and blow him a kiss. The gun and a single bullet were in front of him on a table in a coffee shop. She just disappeared before he could say anything. He really never knew why he saved the gun and the bullet. He just knew that now they had made him the walking dead or worse. He spit and stood up. He was not dead or at least his body wasn't. He felt his head to find the bullet wound that should have killed him. It wasn't there. Either he was insane or something abnormal was happening to him. He now was homeless and smelled bad. He was wearing dead people's clothes that didn't even match. He needed to find someone that could help him. His mind raced

He remembered a bank that he had hidden some of his payments from his kills. He was thinking that there were more. Lawrence was now alive and now had to find a way to understand how he was standing on a street corner after shooting himself in his head. He just needed to remember the bank and how to get the money out. He stood up and walked toward he was not sure where. He seemed to know the way though. That was what he couldn't understand. He needed to find the woman. The one who gave him the gun and the bullet. He walked into a bank and after many questions because he had no ID, he withdrew four thousand dollars. He would now look for the woman that gave him a gun and a bullet. The problem was she was in a fog when he met her. He never thought about how odd it was that she just showed up at a coffee shop he was in and left a gun and a bullet. He was on a job at the time. He just took them and hid them in his clothes. He saved them though. That was the problem. He kept them and tried to end his life with them. It didn't happen. Now he needed to know why? He walked out of the bank with no clue as to where he was going. He was looking for a mystery woman. She was definitely a mystery to him. He just walked around confused and not sure where he would end up. He sat down on a street corner wondering if he was ever going to understand what had happened to him. He wept. He was totally lost! He took off the mismatched sneakers and threw them into the oncoming traffic.

He then stood up and went to a hotel that he didn't remember.

"Welcome back Mr Lloyd."

The Porter knew him. He just walked past him and went to the front desk.

"Mr Lloyd it has been a while."

Lawrence just didn't know what was happening.

"My regular room and someone that can get me some new clothes."

"As you wish."

The clerk gave him a key card to room 666. He took it and headed for the elevator. He didn't know how or why he was in this hotel, but it might give him some clue as to who he was. He hoped so. Lawrence was going to find out that there was life after death. He used the only gun that couldn't kill him with the only bullet that could make him understand that he was special. He would now face his past. Most people never got this special treatment. Lawrence would now find out who he was. He had been given a gun and a bullet that would change his life forever. Lawrence was about to relive his past. The witch that gave him the gun and the bullet entered the hotel and went to the elevator. She pressed the button that would take her to room 666. Lawrence turned the shower to hot. He was going to wash himself. He just didn't know who would walk out of the shower. He never thought he would meet the witch that brought him there. She held a towel for him. He just walked around her. He was now not alive. He died and was resurrected on a table in the morgue. He was now facing a person that he needed to meet. She smiled at him. She blew him a kiss. She had done so once before.

Now he was going to try and remember that moment. A moment in a coffee shop. He accepted her kiss. He just wished he had saved the toe tag so he could throw it in her face. He only remembered a moment that he never thought he would remember. She just blew him another kiss. He would now pay for his sins. She walked toward the door to the hotel room and turned toward him.

"You will find Hell! You are just beginning your journey!"

She closed the hotel room door.

Lawrence knew he was fucked. The woman that gave him the gun wanted more than his soul. He guessed she wanted him to pay for the souls he had killed.

He fell to his knees and sputtered these words.

"I am not a person that can be forgiven."

He was about to face his maker. He just didn't know who his maker was?

He was about to find out though.

The woman he needed answers from just shut the door on him.

He opened the door to his hotel room and fell to his knees. He saw her standing in front of the elevator.

"I just want you to understand me."

She shrugged her head and entered the elevator.

"I gave you a choice once and you tried to kill yourself with it. You are on your own from now on."

The elevator door closed.

Lawrence now figured out that he was going to see his life unfold before him. He couldn't die until he understood why he was who he had become.

THE MORGUE

Lawrence went back into the room and closed the door. On the coffee table was the same gun and a bullet. He fumbled toward the coffee table and loaded the gun with the one bullet. He held it to his head and pulled the trigger. The gunshot sound was loud and clear. Lawrence held the gun in his hands just looking at it. He had failed again to kill himself with the gun and bullet. Lawrence was now laying on a stainless steel table in a morgue. Lawrence screamed. He looked down at his feet. He wore a toe tag. He was dying all over again

Writer note:

Children are easily led toward the inquisitive side of the universe and they want to learn about the past and the future if they can. This is a story that deals with a young child's imagination leading him to a discovery. This could be our future! This is one of the last forty year ago stories that I wrote. It is a little confusing because the characters are having trouble understanding each other. They are living lives that are centuries or double centuries apart. I just thought it would amuse you if you feel that you are still a child. I am just saying? the future may not be all you think it will be. Children are still wanting to learn.

THE JUNGLE

MOST OF US TODAY DON'T know about the future, or the past for that matter, but Josh, well he knows a little about everything. I remember listening to his tales for long periods of time on how it was and what it was like to live in a primitive society. Hell, it even sounded like it was fun. He fondly called these times "the jungle." I only have so much time here, so let me tell you what I learned!

"Sammy, as he now calls me, I want to tell you about the jungle" as he would say, and of course just being a child, I would become his captive audience for as long as he could talk which sometimes was for extended periods of time.

As I said earlier, Josh knew a little bit about everything and by listening to him I learned a little bit about everything myself. The jungle though was the one thing that I couldn't hear enough about. It was so unbelievable and Josh seemed to glow when he talked about it. This is just one of his stories.

"Sammy, did I ever tell you how the jungle came to it's end?"

"I didn't? Well, it started many years before our world was even discovered. There weren't even spaceships and matter transferors then. They didn't even have the technology to produce thought projectors. I was just a boy when I lived there, but I still remember it well. My pals and I used to watch our parents and secretly wondered how they had grown up without television and jet airplanes. They were so ignorant compared to us. In fact when they told us that we were very lucky to have a nice house to live in and plenty of food to eat, we would just laugh to ourselves and dream about flying around the world or traveling to outer space. Our parents were very naive and that is what we never wanted to become. We feared living a dull and routine life where nothing new happened or even had a chance to begin. Our parents had no idea that we were so into our own little world that theirs no longer mattered to us. They worried about gasoline, a fossil fuel, and we didn't even know where it came from or why it was so important to them. We wondered about who would become the next movie star or if a new planet would be discovered by scientists. And much to our regret, our parents made us go to schools that tried to teach us things that we could care less about. Yes, Sammy, those were some very rough times for us kids. But of course the jungle wasn't all backward by any means. No, that is where we got our inspiration to create a new world. You see, we always believed that nothing can grow if it remained motionless and that is why we created the new world. The jungle was a motionless planet. It couldn't move. Everyone had to remain where they were in the universe. Well, let me tell you when anything cannot move then something or someone must move it. Our new world had its roots in the jungle because that is where we were born but we wanted to leave the jungle and that is why it finally came to it's end. The children killed it. They found it's main fault and then corrected it. Now this was not an easy task. The parents didn't know that the kids had so much knowledge about things that they could not understand or even could try to understand. The children learned about four times faster than any generation in the past because they were being raised on fantasy and science fiction which their parents didn't even consider as an education. The jungle was concerned about the past and the present and we kids knew nothing moving could come from that. So, when the planet finally found itself in motion and all of its inhabitants had to learn new ways in order to survive it was a marvelous time for we kids. All the old schools were closed and centers were opened where anyone who learned something new could educate others.

Everyone was important and things like gasoline and food were just used for experimentation. Drugs and matter transferors took the spotlight. What once was thought to be science fiction became reality. Children were creating new organisms and finding ways to make life fun. I remember coming to one of the centers and telling the adults and other children about a water substitute I created. It was at that point in my life that the greatest thrill that I could ever imagine happened to me. I demonstrated how a person could take regular air and turn it into a jelly that was as nourishing as a glass of water. You see, water was the ingredient that made up most of the forms that lived in the jungle. I was a hero and was given privileges that only the most creative discoverers were given. I was then allowed to discover space travel and it changed me forever. Anyway, back to how the jungle came to an end. Like I told you, I was just a child mind you, but I was old enough to realize that something was happening that I should be a part of. I was constantly hanging out with my friends and one day we decided to form a club where we would be required to find something new to share with the others each day. It was hard but fun and we all took it very seriously. Soon other clubs began to form and a competition began to see which club was the most creative. Since we were the first club, we were the club to beat. Our club took the name Atlantis, a legendary civilization in the jungle, the others followed suit. Soon the competition became furious by challenging each other to discovery sessions. The clubs would bring the jungle to it's end. The kids found a better way to educate themselves and nothing could be done to stop them from continuing their education. The funny thing was that the jungle didn't even realize it was a jungle. The kids didn't even start calling it the jungle until many years later. For now it was their home planet. They also only cared about beating their rival club for that week. The whole idea became big business. The television stations started broadcasting the discovery sessions. The discoveries traveled so fast across the jungle that soon a modern world that no one could dream of became a reality. The clubs were making adults look like monkeys, a hairy little animal once believed to be the origin of intelligent life in the jungle. Adults started to attack the clubs and tried to stop the broadcasts. It was of no use though, as the kids outnumbered the adults by a large margin and were easier to mobilize. The adults were forced to either join a club or form clubs of their own. It truly was a new world. The adults began to learn the new ways and it changed their lives. The kids were learning so fast that they started experimenting with moving the jungle. That was when the jungle was forced out of its present position in the universe. It was made mobile."

Now when Josh got to talking about the jungle he would sometimes get side tracked and talk about things that weren't exactly what he started talking about. By this I mean that when he was telling me about how the jungle came to an end he would stray off track and start talking about how it was to live in the jungle. Don't get me wrong, Josh wasn't absent-minded or anything like that, he just sometimes got carried away when he was talking about the jungle. This story will be told just the way Josh told it to me. So, if you get a picture of how it was to live in the jungle then you will have gotten a bonus. This particular story deals with the way the jungle came to an end. I just interrupted the story to let you know that this story will probably be a long drawn out story because Josh really liked the jungle and when it ended he was heart broken. Now back to the story about how the jungle came to an end. Josh spoke again.

"Sammy those pals of mine and all the other kids that formed the clubs, well we kind of became celebrities. We were allowed to experiment with all kinds of newly invented gadgets and discoveries and soon invented the first matter transferor which was the beginning of what future worlds are using now. Now how the jungle was forced out of its original orbit is something else. You see all sorts of experiments were being conducted to find alternate energy sources and one time when a combination of these experiments was being tried, BOOM! The jungle just took off as if it was a space ship. Well, let me tell you something. Everyone on the jungle thought that this was the end. Total panic was widespread across the jungle. No one was sure how much air there was surrounding the jungle or how long it would last. Everyone was running around confused and frightened. Nothing was being done about finding out what could be expected by the jungle being thrust into motion. No one was now anyone after the jungle became mobile. Atlantis was about the safest place for me and my pals to go to. So that is where we headed. That is when we kids had to take control and eventually cause the jungle to come to an end. Panic was so widespread and people were starting to kill each other. Gangs of people were moving all over the jungle looting and burning everything that they encountered. Most of the kids were safe in their clubs and became the only humans that were thinking somewhat rational. They took over the communications and broadcast warnings were sent to the looters. The clubs then formed centers based on the original centers and tried to find some answers to what was happening to the jungle. The clubs dissolved because the centers were now where the knowledge that was needed would have to come from. Only a few people did not come to these centers with their discoveries. These were scientists that became known as the "astronauts." They had found a way to guide the jungle through space unbeknown to the rest of the jungle's population. They finally came to the centers and recruited the brightest and best of the kids. They then introduced them to space ships manned by the true state's chosen few in the jungle. My grand parents were some of these chosen few known as astronauts."

Josh seemed lost in thought for a moment, then continued telling to the story.

"Now Sammy when I first got to see a space ship I was like a little baby.

Even after all of the discoveries and all the organization I had to do I just couldn't believe someone had found a way to leave the jungle and not worry about having to come back to it. These scientists, the astronauts, discovered that the jungle was a giant space ship protected by its atmosphere and was perfectly capable of keeping the jungle alive as long as it did not get too damaged by objects in space. They had found ways to control the jungle's mobility. They knew that eventually the jungle would collide with an object of similar size though and that would be the end of the jungle. The jungle was only a safe haven for a limited time and they were producing smaller versions of the jungle so that they could leave the jungle before it was destroyed. They had to keep a great number of the jungle's populace in the dark so they had time to produce enough of these ships to save as many people as possible. These ships were the ancestors of the new cities that would be formed after the jungle died. If these astronauts hadn't discovered a way to produce these ships then we kids wouldn't be alive and you never would have existed. I was one of the first to test these ships and actually the first to pilot one of these ships off of the jungle. When I think of how these ships formed the first cities in the new world, I just cry. They were remarkable pieces of machinery. You see Sammy, I was part of the reason the jungle came to an end. I from the day I was born thought of it only as my home planet. To me everything that happened that drove people mad or made them plunder and loot only made me work harder to leave the jungle and start a new world. I as a child was allowed to work with the astronauts and even test the first space ships capable of leaving the jungle behind. Yes, we kids killed the jungle. But to we kids nothing was permanent and if it could not move then someone or something had to make it mobile. The jungle was doomed the day we were born. We as kids could not allow anything that had the potential to grow remain motionless. We through our clubs and then our centers made the adults turn over the jungle to us. We then through our experiments accidentally made the jungle grow and as with all growing things the jungle would have to come to an end. You see the jungle came to an end for a good cause. It had to end for our new world to be formed. The jungle ended the way our new world began, it became mobile and thus was allowed to grow. In our new world everything was mobile because that is the way we created it. Our world had to be created because the jungle could no longer stay motionless. After the jungle came to an end we wandered in space for many years until we figured out how to construct the new worlds. We constructed them so that they could never come to an end the way the jungle did. So you see Sammy the jungle ended in a very interesting way. If it wasn't for people like me though no one would know the jungle ever existed. You see, when the jungle ended as did everything that was immobile."

At this point Josh was getting very tired so I used my thought projector to send me back into his globe. You see, Josh is just a memory that I found one day while I was cleaning out an old globe storage facility. In our world we don't have forms like those of the past worlds. We are only sources of energy that drift through space and we move our energy through what we call matter transferors. Our only pleasure comes from our ability to use our thought projectors, and through them we can relive any part of the past that was sealed into memory like globes like Josh. Josh is one of the oldest that I have discovered, but I am only a child and this is my first universe to search. I will only be allowed a certain amount of time in this universe before I will be required to move on to further my education. I am still amazed at how immobile Josh's world was because anything that cannot move has to be moved by someone or something. That is the only way for anything to grow. Josh told me a good story though.

Writer note:

Most people are happy to live a prosperous life. But, what if you wanted more and when you got it you wanted more. Now in the real world women are mostly seen as persons that need protecting. Men fall for this ruse more often than not, but what if there was a woman that just wanted to be on top all the time. This little story is about one such woman. She just couldn't get enough. Now she will see where that leads her. Being on top doesn't mean you win!

FEMALE

Ross Perkins is stoned. He just smoked some weed that he was growing in his backyard. He is a failure in life. He moved to the big island of Hawaii to get away from his failed life. The seeds that produced the marijuana he grows were originally flown in from Guatemala or Panama. He could care less. He just wants a buzz and to get so stoned as to forget about the real world. He isn't even sure that there is a real world anymore. People buy his weed and that pays his rent. He takes a few more tokes on the joint that he has rolled. Pipes are the main way of smoking pot on the island but he is going old school today. He is, after all, a child of the sixties. He tries to focus as the smoke rises into the clear blue sky. His neighbors will not like his breaking the rules. He stands and removes his pants and moons no one in particular. He is so stoned that he falls face first onto a lava created driveway. He laughs loud and hard and then speaks!

"God created man and then he went one step further. He created a female." Ross awakes face down in his driveway with his pants down.

He is seeing an island woman. She came to Hawaii with her parents via San Diego. Her name is Saffron, a rare spice. He never understood the island rules because he was an outsider or haole. The people on the Big Island would either accept him or not. He had broken too many of the rules and was now unwelcome to most Hawaiian families because he showed up at Hawaiian meetings as an uninvited haole. He wanted to become a Hawaiian but he was too white. He was given the right to smoke Hawaiian pot though. Pot was his entrance into the Hawaiian culture on the big island. He got stoned the Hawaiian way. Pot on the big island was controlled by the old guard. You either married into the family or you bought in. If you bought in you were not from the island but from a destination to be sent to. Ross was now a pothead that didn't belong. Saffron tried to make Ross a part of the big island's income. He was growing and selling his version of pot. He was so stoned that he didn't understand that Saffron owned him. He took another toke on the joint he didn't remember rolling. Pussy made him a slave. God must be a woman was all he could think of at the moment. Ross then walked into the swimming pool and drowned himself.

Saffron had won. Ross had met his female. Saffron decided that she could fuck her way to the top on the big island. It was not really a big island, but she was cute and this island catered to cute. That made the island smaller. She hooked up with a pot dealer by the name of Kono. Yeah, that was his real name? Half of the big island named their sons Kono.

Hawaiians!

Saffron was a good fuck. Women in Hawaii were rated by how good they fucked or if they could produce children. What else was there to do? Saffron was a good fuck but didn't want to produce children. Saffron did want to become someone on the Big Island though. Ross was dead and she was now with Kono. She would move on. Hawaii would now become her oyster. She would open up her legs to anyone that could give her a future. She cleaned out Ross's apartment and moved in with Kono. Kono didn't beat her and understood that she was not Hawaiian or a haole. She was Saffron. That was enough for him now.

MOTHERS

Now Hawaiian women are considered sacred. They make the babies. Islands are not like any other place in the world. They are isolated and each person on them must find a way to survive. Babies that live past infancy must either figure out how to survive on a island or die. Sometimes they are killed just because someone's family doesn't want any rivals for food. Saffron was no fool. She cuddled with Kono's family and finally fucked his father. She wanted to become family. After she had his father she looked toward the next family that she needed to conquer to gain a seat in Hawaiian lore. She was the female that all hoped would never come to Hawaii. She was the one woman that no island woman wanted to see land on it's shore. She was female. Even Pele knew of her. She was not welcome, yet now she was here. All the mothers on the island joined in prayer. It would be of no use though, as Female had finally landed on the Big Island.

SAFFRON

Saffron was fucking both Kono's father and him. Hawaiians have a long history of incest. Children were only special if they lived past twenty years of age. Saffron didn't give a shit. Kono's father was royalty. That meant she was fucking the past and the future. She wasn't haole or Hawaiian. She was just Saffron. She was special because she was white, beautiful, and not related to anyone on the islands. She was just a good fuck on the big island. You couldn't ask for more than this in this day and age on the big island. She knew she had to fuck her way to the top. Saffron was the woman that never should have landed on this island. She was going to rule the men there. She was Female! Men couldn't resist her. She was just beginning to find men who would do anything for her. She was becoming the ruling Female. The big island had never seen anything like her before. She kept looking at the biggest drug dealers on the island. She found one who had a son by the name of Horatio. The English had a way of keeping the native Hawaiians thinking about the white man. Saffron wanted them to think about a white Queen. She was and wanted to be the next ruler of men on the islands. She would have to control more than drugs on the islands though. Nothing came or went from the islands without the approval of the docks. She had her eyes set on owning them. She asked Horatio to take her to Honolulu for a wild time. He accepted her invitation. She smiled and licked her lips. Horatio would open doors that needed to be opened if she was to gain control of the ports. Saffron wanted it all. She smiled again and licked her lips. She fucked Horatio so well that he was now putty in her hands. It was now off to Honolulu and the ports.

OPEN THE PORTS

Saffron Licked Horatio's lips and cooed her best coo. She was going to take over the ports that brought everything into Hawaii. Horatio had now met a female. Saffron now felt that she was about to get closer to finding a man who could help her own the islands. She just didn't see Male coming. He was not going to be a fool for a woman. He had been around for way too many females. They all were wanting what he had. He just smiled and watched as Horatio gave up his life to this little whore. He owned the docks and many women on the islands. He had heard about Saffron and was happy that she was coming to Honolulu to try and take what he owned. He would set a trap for her. He wanted to own her. She was a female that needed to be watched as she controlled men more easily than most females he had met in the past. But Male was in charge and Female would always just be his whore. Saffron was now about to meet a Male she had never thought could exist. The male's name was Vincent. He was a killer and didn't hide the fact. If anyone cared, he just had them killed. He just ruled. It was that simple. Saffron was now about to find out if she truly was "FEMALE."

MALE

Saffron had horatio catering to her every wish. She had no idea there was a male like Vincent in charge. Vincent drank champaign and looked out at the ocean from his patio. He was the chosen Male to control the docks. Males were the dominant people on the islands. A female like Saffron was rare and like her name a spice to be savored. Vincent was not sure what he wanted to do with her. She was a Female that he smelled and she seemed confident that she could rule the islands. She was a white bitch that had taken many an island boy's soul. He sucked in his breath and let her arrive in Honolulu. He was not going to become a fool. Female would now enter his life. Vincent was about to meet Female! Vincent would wait until he met her before he chose her fate.

Vincent smelled her long before she entered his home. He was the King of the islands. Pussy was not new to him. This pussy smelled different though. She was too sweet a fruit. He had never eaten the forbidden fruit and now he was about to meet it. Saffron walked onto his balcony and sat down and spread her legs. Vincent was now just another male that Female wanted to own.

"Pour me some champaign." She spoke like she owned the islands already!

Vincent dismissed Horatio like he was garbage. Horatio left as quickly as he could.

Saffron spread her legs like she wanted to be eaten like the forbidden fruit she was selling. Vincent shot her four times in her chest and head just to make sure that was enough to kill her. He was the Male on these islands. Too many Females tried to take his place. He just put another one down. He kissed his smoking gun and shot her again just to make sure that she was dead. He ruled the docks and the islands! "Female" was now shark food.

WRITER NOTE:

There are many stories about royals. Many are about how they kill each other off to gain the throne. Incest, rape, poisonings, and of course the occasional dagger in the back. All are probably true and happened sometime and someplace in history. Well, here is one such story. It just doesn't follow any of the old scripts. This throne will scare people. It is just a story though, so don't think power over people is just a royal. It just might be the throne itself.

THE THRONE

MEGAN

FREDERICK HAD A DAUGHTER WITH a pagan girl he took while roaming in the woods with his guards one day. She never thought about being in his kingdom though because he never went back to that part of the woods again. He just produced another bastard that he didn't know about. He didn't give her mother money to live by because she never went to his castle or told anyone but her daughter who her father was. Megan was a forgotten child. She was now eighteen years old and knew who her father was. She stared at the castle and hissed.

"I will not be a whore or a woman that can be controlled by a man. I will kill you father if I ever meet you! You just discarded my mother like she was nothing!"

Megan was becoming a woman. She did not want what most women wanted. A life of being taken cared of. She stared at the castle and wondered how she could find a man to make her free of living in a forest? She hated the castle and everyone in it. She was the perfect fit to become the new royal. She just didn't know it. Neither did Frederick. He was old and dying. He was looking for a man to take his place. Megan was more than any man he could ask for. Frederick called for his fortune teller. He was now desperate to find a successor.

Megan went to the village and drank a beer as she sized up the men at the bar. She would sleep alone tonight.

Royals in Frederick's family had inbred for centuries. Most of the children left in his line of succession were now either idiots, poets, or totally mad. Either way, none of them were fit to succeed him when he died. Someone would have to assume his throne though. He had lived a long and violent life. Frederick was an old king. He was dying and he knew it. Who was he going to allow to assume the throne? It didn't seem that anyone in his immediate family or for that matter any of the rest of his family were not capable of ruling or wanted the job. Even his bastard sons and daughters were not willing to come forth and try to rule. He sat on his throne in deep thought. His hand was clenched in a fist and he was leaning on a sword just staring out into the throne room. He would have to find someone whom he could put on the throne. This throne room was not given to him. He murdered, raped, and bought his way to it. He now looked out at an empty room. He had no one to talk to about his death. He was just a old man that had killed everyone that could have given him peace in his final hours. He was finally scared. He had no idea what was going to happen to him. He was not awaiting a good death. He kept staring out at the throne room wondering when it would ask him to gasp his last breath? His fortune teller entered the throne room. Frederick unclenched his hand but kept a firm grip with his other hand on his sword. He felt a breeze blow and the smell of a woman entering the throne room. He stared at his fortune teller and spoke.

"What is my fate?"

FREDERICK

FREDERICK SAT ON HIS THRONE aching in his old age. He needed someone to take his throne. He was being scrutinized by every idiot in the kingdom. He didn't want to give up his throne to someone who could not rule.

His fortune teller came to him. He told him that his successor would be a woman. Frederick remembered smelling a woman enter the throne room when the fortune teller came in. He held his breath and listened as the fortune teller spoke.

"She is of your bloodline. She is a pagan. She doesn't want the throne. She will only gain it by killing you. She will become a Queen. Your kingdom will become hers. She is your daughter. You just never met her. You still will die by her sword. You will create a Queen that the people will worship. Her name is Megan."

Frederick laughed loud and hard.

"I am to be replaced by a woman?"

He coughed hard and spit blood.

"I hope she kills me with the first blow. I just want to die like a King."

His fortune teller spoke again.

"You will die like a dog. She will kill you while the court watches. She will take the throne by force. She will be known as a Queen. She will kill you like the life you lived, violently."

The fortune teller told him he would die like a dog. He believes he deserves such a death. Now he will have to face it but to be replaced by a woman is more than he ever thought could happen to him. He clenches his fist again and raises his sword into to the air and shouts.

"I am the King and this throne is mine. It will have to be taken from me by killing me!"

JUDGEMENT DAY

FREDERICK SITS ON HIS THRONE for almost forty eight hours just staring out at the room. He proclaimed he would name his successor the first day after the next full moon. He is scared but isn't willing to show his fear. He is awaiting an unpleasant death. He is afraid to sleep. He had always been so confident that he was in control. Now he was just a fool sitting on a throne that had been around for centuries and he was just a tenant. He now understood that the throne was all that mattered. His occupying it for his reign was just a whiff of smoke in time. He looked hard and long at the throne room. He was seeing it for the last time in his putrid horrible life. He had done so many horrible things while he sat on the throne. He was about to pay the throne it's dues. It wanted a ruler that made it something more than a monster. He was now supposed to name his successor. It was going to end his life as King and if the fortune teller was speaking the truth about putting a Queen in his place that would make the throne become a place that everyone would want to rise to. Frederick was seeing that his life was of no purpose. He had failed to sit upon the throne as a good King.

MEGAN ENTERS THE THRONE ROOM

THE THRONE ROOM WAS FILLED with Frederick's ill bred and whatever. Megan gained entrance by accompanying the fortune teller who found her in the woods. He led her to the front of the motley crowd awaiting to see who Frederick would pick as his successor. Megan removed her cloak and rushed the throne.

Frederick looked old, sick and tired. Megan looked him in his eyes.

"I curse you and anyone that calls you a father. You are worse than a pig's shit. I am your daughter and I will kill you like the dog you are."

She drew her sword and walked up to Frederick.

"Die you asshole!"

She slit his throat. He did die like a dog. Megan threw him from the throne like she would throw a bone to a dog. Megan took the throne and smiled at the people there.

The people in the throne room bowed down and shouted, "The King is dead, long live the Queen!"

Megan now spoke as a Queen.

"Now we will make this throne something that matters."

It now mattered little that it was not an evil man that was in charge. A woman was now the person people would ask favors from. Megan took a throne she never wanted. The throne took it's next victim. Megan was now on trial!

A queen was born!

She was on trial!

WRITER NOTE

The western world has always entered the third and fourth worlds and attempted to conquer them. All they really accomplished was to become a spectator. They look at these places as if they were just filled with savages. Most of these places have jungles and the inhabitants there find a way to survive in them. Westerners always are just visitors. They are really not welcome but become accepted because of money and trade. The westerners will return home eventually and the jungles will go back to what they really are, jungles. This story still makes me hide under the covers. I don't want to travel to remote places anymore. Read this story and maybe you won't want to either. Maybe there is a jungle in front of me right now and I just don't want to see it? I just found the one I didn't want to find! Jungles are everywhere. We just need to see them! I met the new jungle and wished I didn't find it. This story is not for beginners. Beware!

THE NEW JUNGLE

THE FIRST STOP

Marco awoke sweating from a nightmare. He remembered that he was fearing for his life. His new wife Sydney, kissed him and rubbed up against him. He felt aroused and she jumped him. They had sex. Marco was not thinking clearly because of the sex. He was awakened from a nightmare though and he knew that much. He had to think. Sex was clouding his mind. What did he see in his nightmare? Sex erased his memory of the nightmare. He was lost. He had no memories of his dream. Sex with Sydney was magical. It made him a fool. All he could think of was when he would have sex with her again. Nightmares were just that. Nightmares. Or was this one different?

Marco was on his honeymoon. He was going to travel to many remote places on the planet. His parents were wealthy and bought tickets to many remote areas of the world for his honeymoon. They wanted his new wife and him to experience places that were very isolated from the civilized world. They wanted him to see the world the way they saw it. Sydney was studying primitive societies and Marco and she were to visit the most primitive places on the planet on this honeymoon. They were now on Bora Bora, Tahiti. They were staying in a cabin that had glass floors so they could see the fish and reefs below them. He stood up and felt dizzy. He wasn't sure that his nightmare was over. He looked down and saw a reef shark eat a fish. This really was a primitive spot on the planet. Sydney wanted more sex. Marco stared at the shark as he left the floor and returned to the bed. Sex always seemed to make everything seem all right. Marco was now the shark. Sydney was his prey.

After sex they both fell into the bed and panted. Both were satisfied. Marco remembered that there was a funeral taking place as they landed on Bora Bora. Sydney lay on the bed and rolled over as if she wanted to sleep. Marco arose and pulled a tapestry that the male locals wore around their waist and left the room. He walked down the wooden pier and entered the jungle. He heard voices. He crept as silently as he could toward the voices. He then witnessed what he could only describe as a waking nightmare. The person that had been in the funeral was now being consumed as dinner for the island elite. The locals were eating the dead person. Protein was not always so easily gotten on an island. The ritual he was witnessing was just something the island had accepted as normal. He looked at the people gathered around for the feast. He felt that he was going to vomit but he held it in an backed into the jungle. He then puked and sat down for what seemed like hours to him. He thought he saw his wife eating a dead person. He then ran for his room and Sydney. He wanted to leave this island tonight. He knew there were no planes coming or leaving until tomorrow though. He crawled into the bed and heard Sydney breathing her sleep breaths. He pulled the sheet over his head and hoped that a sunrise would come soon. He wanted to get off Bora Bora. He just witnessed what primitive really meant. He wanted to go somewhere else. Anywhere else. He smelled blood coming from Sydney's breath. He wasn't ready for this. Sydney was not who he thought she was. She was a cannibal.

FIJI

Marco held Sydney's hand and dragged her to the entrance of the airport. He was sweating and Sydney noticed that he was not acting like a rational person.

"Stop!"

Sydney grabbed Marco and hugged him.

"You are scaring me!"

She then asked?

"Tell me what is wrong?"

Marco looked Sydney in her eyes and said. "We are not safe!"

Sydney hugged him and spoke into his ear.

"We can deal with this!"

They landed in Fiji and left the airport and were now in their hotel room. Marco spoke in a frenzied voice.

"I saw people eating a corpse on Bora Bora."

Sydney sucked in her breath and then spoke.

"Why did you not tell me about this?"

"I was afraid that you would think I was losing my mind."

Sydney hugged Marco hard and spoke into his ear again.

"I will make the nightmares about the islands that we are traveling to seem like a voyage."

Marco held her at arms length.

"I am afraid for both of us."

She spoke in a calm and a almost comatose voice.

"We are going to take a journey that will not make much sense in the modern world. I think that we are about to see a world that is not exactly normal. Your parents bought us a pass to the unknown parts of the world. I as a scientist want to see what awaits us. You as a discoverer will have to adapt.

"Tonight we will shrink a person's head. Come my love into a world of the unimaginable."

Marco was now understanding why his parents arranged his marriage to Sydney. He now knew that he had become a partner in a journey that his parents so graciously gave them because they were like Sydney. He was their prisoner. He was now going to have to kill all of them.

"I saw you eat some of that person who died on Bora Bora!"

Sydney spoke.

"I was not asleep when you saw the island's elite eating that person. I ate a part of him. I was there."

Marco's face became pale. Sydney was not the woman he thought she was. He pushed her away and stared at her. She had eaten part of a human being. He vomited. She just looked at him and spoke.

"You must accept that the world is filled with unimaginable things. Your parents have given us a free ride to discover the wonders that have been hidden. Fiji has shrunken heads. Let us see how they do it?"

Most shrunken heads are from the central portion of South America. Marco and Sydney were now going to see how the islands produced them. Fiji was now going to show them a horror that only an island that was far from civilization could produce. Marco walked away from Sydney. He then turned and screamed at her."

"You are a monster. I don't want anything to do with you!"

She just laughed loud and hard.

"You are a fool! I fuck you and you think that the world is a safe place. The world is filled with evil things and the people that live in most places are nothing more than animals. There are some of us that have found out how to control these animals. We are the future. Your parents are not so innocent that they sent us on a vacation to discover new lands. They sent us on a discovery mission. They know that only some of us will inherit the future. They wanted me to educate you. You are just a child to the next rulers of this planet. You will either wake up to what is real or I will have to kill you."

Marco strangled Sydney and spit on her. She was now just a piece of meat laying on a beach in Fiji.

He really did see her eat some of that person on Bora Bora. He just couldn't accept it and had tried to erase it from his memory. He now knew that she and his parents would need to be erased from this world. He booked a flight back to San Francisco. He would kill his parents and anyone else that he thought was part of the order that thought they were in control. The new jungle was coming home.

Marco got off the plane at the San Francisco airport and ran as fast as he could away from everything that seemed like authority. He would soon be charged with the murder of Sydney. He wanted to disappear. He was now on borrowed time. He had to kill the people that wanted him to join them. He took all the money out of his wallet and threw his wallet away. He was now going to have to become a homeless person. The world was now Just a place that a person had to find a hiding place in for him. He traded one jungle for another. He found a next jungle and hoped it was safer than the one he was supposed to see. Marco was now just another animal in the world. He ran as fast as he could. He had nowhere to run to though. He stopped and tried to get his breath back. He looked around. He was now on the streets. He had found the jungle his parents never wanted him to find. Welcome to the new Jungle! He put his hands over his face to hide his eyes. He was now in a place that no parent would ever wish upon their son. He was now on his own and would have to kill the people that made him. He was in a new jungle. He had become an animal that needed to kill to survive. He would have to do it in this jungle though. His parents no longer were paying the bill. Marco was going to have to understand this new jungle. He was now a animal in a jungle he never thought could exist. He looked around. He was now all alone. He smiled and walked toward nowhere. He truly was alone. But he was in a jungle his parents would never look for him in. He would find a way to kill them. After all, he was now just another animal looking for a meal.

He welcomed the "New jungle." It was now his new world!

WRITER NOTE

Sometimes when you are desperate fate or whatever takes over and makes you forget that you are really seeing reality wrong. Frank is about to find out that giving up is not the answer but a choice. He will find out the bottom can still go lower. He will just have to have his night on the town. Frank will find out that he never was the center of this universe. There is a place that wants him to go to. It is the elevator to Hell. He will have his "Night on the town." The elevator button is pressed for Hell. He just wasn't looking for that trip.

NIGHT ON THE TOWN

FRANK ENTERS HARRAHS IN LAKE Tahoe a little desperate. He has about $1500 dollars on him. It is the last of the money he has in his checking account. He is so nervous and uncomfortable that he heads to the first bar he sees to get a drink to settle his nerves. He sits down next to one of the most beautiful women he has ever seen. She has long red hair and a body that a goddess would be jealous of. He nods to her and she flashes him a smile that seems to gleam like diamonds. He then motions for the bartender to come over to him. The girl next to him speaks in a very sexy husky sounding voice. "Would you like a night on the town?"

"I am Jezebel. How about me showing you a night on the town?"

Frank's jaw drops and he is sure that it will hit the bar. All he can do is cough out a "I'm Frank and I would love to join you for a night on the town."

"Good, but I meant I want to treat you to a night on the town."

His jaw drops again. He can not believe this is happening to him.

"You want to treat me to a night on the town?"

"That is what I said."

She then glides over and sits on the stool next to him.

Frank isn't the most handsome guy in the world and yet not that unattractive either, but he just couldn't believe this was happening to him. She had to be a ten plus and he was between a six and eight. The bartender comes over and Frank orders a double Dewars on the rocks.

"Put it on my tab, purred Jezebel, and gives the bartender a $50 dollar bill. She then purred. Close out my account and keep the change."

She then turned her full attention toward Frank and purred at him waving ten $100 dollar bills. "Are you ready for your night on the town?"

"Are you a whore?"

She laughs in her sexy husky voice and speaks.

"I'm just a woman that wants to show you a night on the town."

Frank has no more questions. He is caught up in the web that Jezebel is weaving and is ready and willing. He walked into Harrahs not really sure of himself or where he was heading and now he was being offered a night on the town by a beautiful temptress. He got his scotch and gulped it down. He is ready for his night on the town.

South Tahoe is not a large town and it is split between California and Nevada. It does have its bright spots and he wanted to see all of them. Jezebel then leans over and kisses him deeply. She then grabs his hand and pulls him from the bar stool. She leads him toward the front door of Harrahs. He was now going to see the town the way Jezebel wanted him to see it. He is no longer in control. Tahoe is now a paradise to him. Frank gives in totally to Jezebel. He wants what Jezebel wants to give him. It was like he is giving his soul to her. He is now going to see the town the way Jezebel wants him to see it. Tahoe will now become a paradise to him. Frank gives in totally to Jezebel. He forgets why he was so depressed and at rock bottom in his life.

Jezebel leads Frank out of Harrahs. He isn't drunk but he feels like he might be. Jezebel is in control. He follows her like she is going to tell him a secret that he wants to hear. He looks her in the eyes and then becomes her slave. She wants him to enjoy what she is giving him. She speaks.

"I am going to give you a night on the town!"

Frank is mesmerized. He really never had a night out on the town before. Is he ready for one?

He watches as Jezebel leads him out the front door of Harrahs. He thinks he sees a tail under her dress but he just keeps following her.

Jezebel kisses him and a limosine stops and a door opens.

He is now getting his night on the town!

They enter The MGM and go to a craps table. Jezebel throws ten one hundred dollar bills on the table and tells the dealer to give Frank the chips. They gamble until about eleven thirty PM. Jezebel tells Frank it is time to leave. They won some money and Frank is happy and willing to keep following Jezebel.

Frank follows Jezebel to the black limousine. She smooths her dress across her long shapely legs. Frank just looks at her and feels like he doesn't belong here.

Jezebel tells the driver in her sexy voice.

"North Tahoe"

The car leaves Harrahs. It is eleven thirty on a friday night. Frank is getting his night on the town.

ROAD TO NORTH TAHOE

The car weaves along the highway that will lead them to North Tahoe. Jezebel whispers into Frank's ear.

"What is your wildest dream?"

Frank stutters. He never thought about his wildest dream before. He answers.

"I don't have a wildest dream."

Jezebel purrs into his ear again.

"Well it is time that you had one."

She kisses Frank hard and deep letting her tongue penetrate his throat. She removes her tongue from his mouth and smiles into his eyes.

"You just need me to guide you."

Frank is now totally in Jezebel's hands. He wants to have a wildest dream. He thinks he must have fallen into some sort of a dream that he never thought would happen to him. Jezebel just was nothing he ever thought could happen to him. He blinks three times and when he opens his eyes Jezebel is still there and he feels the car traveling on winding roads. He wants his night on the town. He just can't believe that he is getting it.

Jezebel unzips Frank's pants and then pulls his underwear down past his knees. She starts sucking his cock and he loses control. She spits his semen on the floor of the car and Jeszebel continues to suck his cock.

Frank moans as he gets erect again. Jezebel knows what she is doing. She pulls her panties off and mounts Frank. She fucks him like he has never been fucked before. He gasps for breath and then sees that Jezebel has a tail. He pushes her off of him. He speaks.

"What the fuck are you?"

"I am your night on the town you loser."

Frank pulls up his underwear and pants. He then sees that Jezebel is laughing at him. She speaks.

"You wanted to gamble what a pitiful life you were living and I was sent to take it from you. I just was supposed to give you your night on the town before I took your life."

It was now twelve o'clock saturday morning. Her tail enters Frank's mouth and he gurgles his last breath. Jezebel takes his wallet out of his pants pocket and takes the fifteen hundred dollars and his winnings. She tells the driver to drive to the desert and find a place that no one will find Frank's body. He had his his night on the town!

WRITER NOTE

Some people just need a stage. This story is about one of those people. They can only survive by taking the next chance. They have to gamble. Sometimes though the price is tomorrow. Just what will you win if you bet everything and win? This story deals with a person with nothing to lose or win. He is a gambler. He just might not understand what he is gambling for though. That is why we call it gambling. When he beat the Devil did he really win? Gamblers call it a showdown. A cool story!

I LOOKED THE DEVIL
IN THE EYE

I AM A PROFESSIONAL GAMBLER. I mostly play poker. I have been on television many times and have played against some of the best in the business. I am an alcoholic, drug addict, and was married and divorced three times. I have been in and out of so many rehab centers that now when I enter most of them, they wag a finger at me and point toward the door. I am not good for their business. My temper has gotten so bad lately that I am even not getting any television invites anymore. That is why I accepted the invitation to this special poker game.

I walked into the poker room which was in the rear of a small casino off the strip. There he was. Smug! He was just staring at me as I entered the room. There was a table with nine places, yet he was the only person sitting there at the moment.

He was looking at me like I was meat on a plate. I stared into his blood red eyes and shivered. He wasn't going to blink. I didn't know if he knew who I was or if he really cared to. I winked at him and strolled around the table trying to decide where I would sit. I was not going to give him anything. I certainly wasn't going to give him a tell. Poker is not just a game to me. It is a showdown between players. I consider myself a player and most people that I know that become professional gamblers are also. I sat down and winked at him again. I was ready for him and wasn't so sure that he was ready for me.

Soon every seat at the table was occupied. I didn't recognize any of the players but they all seemed to know the man who was seated when I entered the room. I thought this was quite strange because I knew most of the Vegas players. To sit at a table with eight unknowns was just freaking me out a little. I only brought so much money and wasn't even sure what the buy in was. I guess it really didn't matter because if I lost all that I brought then I would just lick my wounds somewhere else.

The man that was sitting at the table all alone when I entered introduced himself.

"I am the Devil. We are going to play for your souls."

Now most normal people would throw up their hands and walk out of the room. I am not normal and I kind of liked the challenge.

"So you claim to be the Devil?" I said very loud!

"I am and you will be playing for your soul."

I stared into his eyes. This guy really thought he was the Devil. I winked and stared into his eyes looking to see if he was just joking. What was I going to do next? I blinked three times and grabbed my balls. I opened my eyes and spoke.

"If you really are the Devil then how did you pick me out to play poker with?"

"You were just the next in line. Sit down and face your future." He smiled as he spoke these words.

I chose a seat next to this guy. I wanted to play after him. I wanted a chance to see if he really had all the cards. Everyone else agreed to play also. I spoke very loud and clear!

"Deal the cards!"

I was sitting at a poker table with a guy who said he was the Devil and seven unknowns in Las Vegas and all I had to bet was my soul. What the Hell did I care? I was going to Hell anyways. It might as well be because of a card game.

My first card was the 2 of spades. I cracked a smile and watched as each player looked at their first card. The Devil didn't bother to look at his. He was staring at me with blood red eyes. I stared back and then smiled again. I was staring the Devil in his eyes. I shot him the finger. It was the only tell I would give him. He didn't move a muscle in his body. We were really playing poker for my soul. I relaxed and waited for my next card. No more middle finger showings.

As I said earlier I am a professional poker player. I have had my share of wins and losses in my career. I never really thought about where my life was heading. Now I was betting I would not enter Hell tonight. The Devil though thought tonight was my time. I looked at him hard and long. He didn't even bother to look at his first two cards. I lifted a corner of my second card. It was the 3 of spades. I spoke to only the guy who was supposed to be the Devil.

"Is this deck rigged?"

He spoke.

"It is just a game of chance with a regular 52 card deck. There is no stacked deck. Your cards are just the same ones that everyone else at the table will receive from a 52 deck of cards."

I have played at tables for many years and know it is about how well a person sees his opponents. I win more often than not because most people are afraid to lose. I am afraid not to win. That has always gotten me to the final table in most tournaments. I just don't want to lose and tonight is no exception. I am staring the Devil in his eyes and I wink. I am not afraid to win. Is he afraid to lose to me? I wink at him again. I speak.

"Keep the cards coming!

The Devil or the man who claims to be him then looks at his cards. He then speaks to the dealer.

"Deal the next card."

I picked up a tell. He didn't have a good hand.

All the people at the table are scared because I can see it in their eyes. I don't know them but I know they are scared and that gives me an advantage. I just don't give a shit and that is my advantage.

I speak.

"I just don't give a shit!"

The Devil or whoever then speaks.

"Then let us play on!"

The next card is dealt.

The Devil or who he claims to be froze just for a moment.

I saw his tell. He was not sure if I was bluffing.

I had him!

He just showed me that I just might win this hand.

The next card was turned up and it was the 5 of spades.

I looked at the man that claimed to be the Devil. He just sat there not giving away what he was thinking which was kind of making me admire him. He was a player even if he claimed that he was just the Devil.

The next card was the King of diamonds.

I sat back and winked at him again. I was giving him a false tell. He spoke.

"Everyone that lasts through this hand can leave with their soul."

Now this was something that disturbed me deeply. I was placing my soul in the pot but what would I win if I won a hand. I knew what I was expected to lose. My soul!

So I am betting my soul and if I win the hand I am just supposed to just walk away? What is the Devil or whoever is giving up? I want to win my soul and something else so that I know that I won something.

I then realized I could save seven other lives. I said.

"Everyone leaves with their souls if I win?"

This made the Devil grin from ear to ear.

"You can name your price. I am not going to cheat you out of a win."

"Anything I want?"

"You can name your price. Souls are worth a lot where I come from."

"Then keep on dealing the cards."

The rest of the table looked at me like I was their spokesperson.

The next card was the 4 of spades.

The Devil stared at me with those blood red eyes and sort of grinned.

I just picked my nose and threw a bugger on the floor. I knew I had him.

"I want you to go to Hell and stay there."

He spoke again.

"Next card please."

The King of clubs showed up.

I had four spades and a straight flush draw but there were two Kings showing. I looked into those blood red eyes of the Devil trying to see his soul, if he had one, but all I could see was darkness. He was staring into my eyes also. We were both trying to see each other's soul. I knew I had one, but did he?

We all received our last card.

I was sort of afraid to look and see what I drew. I was not holding a good hand, but what if I didn't make a flush or a straight. I had only low cards with two Kings showing.

I finally looked the Devil in the eyes and winked. The dealer turned the card over.

It was the Ace of spades. I drew my straight flush.

He turned his down cards over. He had four kings.

I won.

"So now I can get to name my price?"

The Devil looked at me and nodded.

"Then I want you to go back to Hell and never show your face in Las Vegas again!"

He disappeared in a puff of smoke.

I booked a flight to New York. I heard about a game in another back room of a casino. I was sure that I would meet the Devil again. There were just too many back rooms that played poker. Gamblers played poker and would eventually meet the devil. I was going to see him quite often. I was his pupil!

THE CREATURE

WRITER NOTE

AN ALIEN SPACESHIP CRASHES IN a desert in New Mexico. There are many military personnel there discussing weapons of mass destruction. Now scientists are being brought in from all the fields of advanced weapon technology. When a alien spaceship crashes in the area where all these specialists are meeting is not something that the government needs. They rush to the crash site and discover an alien that has died. They rush the corpse to a laboratory and take samples of its DNA. What the scientists do next is going to be classified as Top Secret. Only a few people on this planet will have the clearance to see the files in the future. It still makes a good story though. Think about it? How does the government handle a alien crash landing? I think they will have to make a very hard choice. I as a human though don't know if they can make a right one. This story is about one choice they could choose. What would you do if you were asked to produce a child born of a alien and a human? The government thinks this is just a part of the future. This is just a story! There is no alien DNA being used on pregnant humans, or is what we are being told a lie? I see a story here. Do you?

THE LIEUTENANT

LIEUTENANT CHARLES FRANKLIN WAS ESCORTED into a room with three high ranking military personnel. He was motioned to sit. He followed orders. He was asked if he wanted anything to drink. He sat staring at the high ranked officers in front of him and shook his head no. They stare at him. He starts to sweat. What is he doing here and why was he taken under military guard from his home? He feels like a prisoner being interrogated. He is not far off in his thinking.

A general in the Air Force speaks.

"You are Charles Franklin, a lieutenant in the United States Air Force?"

Charles could do nothing but nod his head. He is not used to being brought before such high ranked military men.

"Your wife is six months pregnant?"

Again all he can do is nod.

"We are going to ask you and your wife to perform a duty for your country. You will be promoted to the rank of full colonel in the Air Force and will be assigned to Washington DC. Are you willing to help out your country?"

Again all he can do is nod.

"You and your wife will be in a program that will be classified as Top Secret. You and she will be under the care of doctors and scientists. You will not be able to speak about what is happening to you to anyone including other family members. You will be living in a special hospital for the time that it takes to finish giving birth to this new child."

Charles head is spinning. He looks at three generals and two admirals and feels like they are up to no good. He stutters as he speaks.

"What are you going to ask of us?"

"We want to inject alien DNA into your wife's baby. We have a dead alien and we want to understand it. We need to get a living specimen. We want you and your wife to breed a alien and human baby. You will never be able to tell anyone what is happening. You will just raise the baby as if it is totally human. We just want to watch it grow and see what it grows into. You will not be able to tell anyone about this except your wife. She must understand that she is going to raise a baby with alien DNA. You have fifteen minutes to decide. After that you will either become a colonel or be sent somewhere that you really don't want to be stationed. This is a one time offer."

He accepts the offer. Being a secret person seems to make him feel special. His wife though has no clue. He has eaten the forbidden fruit. He and his family are now TOP SECRET! How is he going to explain this to his wife? He must though. He calls her and says,"Honey we have to talk!"

THREE YEARS LATER.

Charles and his wife Mary are now living in Springfield, Virginia right off of the Potomac River in a very upper middle class neighborhood. He is a full colonel in the Air Force but has never been given any assignments that made him feel that he is really a full colonel. He is mostly pushing paper in Washington. He is what the military call "The Peter Principal." He is doing his job and collecting a paycheck because there is no other place to put him. He hates his existence. Still he has Mary and his child Buster to think about. Buster is now out of his twos and is entering into the stage of being introduced to other children in schools. Charles knows that the government is watching his child like a star that has just been discovered in outer space for the first time. He has the understanding that he and Mary know that their boy was injected with alien DNA before she gave birth. Both of them fear for their son. He is as normal as any child born human before him, but what will happen if he becomes something different? They go to bed and try to make a new child. Their last child belongs to the government. Charles and Mary just want to be human. They want to create a human baby. They have sex and dream that the last three years never happened. Buster though is real. They fear for him and know that they can't protect him. Buster though is another question. What if he finds out who his real parents are? They shiver under the sheets and make love. They want a human baby. Buster does not belong to them. He is a Top Secret baby.

BUSTER

Buster is growing up in a very upper middle class neighborhood. Buster is going to the best schools in Virginia. He feels that his parents are afraid of him. He sees them glance away and speak in hushed voices sometimes. He sees them with eyes that are not totally human. He sees them as aliens. He is not ready to grow up. He somehow feels that he is not from this planet. He is now six years old though. He sucks in his breath and plays the part of being just a child. He knows something is not right. He is only six years old in human years but his body is telling him that he is much older. His tongue slips out of his mouth and it is forked. He knows he must hide this from his parents and his teachers. He somehow feels like he is not part of this world. In fact he feels like he was sent to this planet on a mission. He decides it is time to reproduce another him. He does so and is not whole anymore. He has produced what the government doesn't want. A human child. He leaves his house and walks along the river toward Washington. He will now do what he was sent to this planet to do. The problem is he had to make a copy of himself. He is now two people. This is a problem for him. He can't think like just a alien because he now sees the world from the eyes of two beings. He is a alien and his double is human. Part of him is walking away from a home he was born into and another that will now have to make sure the other one is not discovered. Buster is a strange child indeed. The first Buster makes himself look like a fish and jumps into the Potomac river. He swims toward the sea. He will just have to discover what he really is. He keeps swimming down a polluted river toward the sea. His other self will function on what kind of a mind he has given it. It will at most be classified as retarded. He can't think about his other self now or his human parents. He must reach the ocean and discover what this planet has to offer the rest of the universe. He was never supposed to be put in this position. His kind just sent him to this planet to try and understand it. Now he will have to find a way to contact his own kind. He is scared because he is now a part of this planet. He is two people. They are just from different planets. He doesn't see any way he can find another one of his species on this planet. He hopes the open ocean is the answer. He swims hard and fast. He has left the human part of him in Virginia. He is now totally a alien in a body he must survive with. He is not two people in one body anymore. He is just a being that crash landed in New Mexico. He will have to go back to where he crash landed his ship if he is able to? There has to be some way to contact his own kind. He swims on not knowing how he will be able to get to his ship. He is totally lost. Swimming to an ocean will not not get him home. He doesn't even know his ship is in a place no ocean can lead him. He keeps swimming and is gaining strength. He is now the alien that landed in the desert in New Mexico. He will have to learn that this is a large planet and he will have to adapt to it. He feels sorry for the person he left behind as Buster in Virginia but he now knows that he is just a alien lost in a world he has no real knowledge of. He keeps swimming toward a ocean that will lead him to nowhere he needs to go. He is lost on a planet that he never should have been sent to. He did leave a human part of himself behind though and that part of him might just become his only hope of finding his kind. He just keeps swimming growing stronger as he swims toward a ocean. His other self just sits down on a floor in his room and moans. He wants his other self to be safe. Buster is a mess. His parents rush to his room and find him pounding his head on the floor and filling his pants up with waste. The other Buster is swimming as fast as he can toward the Atlantic ocean. Government agents rush into the house and find a child they were not expecting. Buster is not the child they need. He is now a mystery and they want to know what happened. Charles and Mary and what is now Buster are rushed to a facility in Washington DC. They are now suspects in an escape of a alien. This is not the child they knew as Buster. All the new tests prove the Buster in the facility is totally human. The trouble is no one knows what happened to the alien part of the child they had bred. The Busters will never be totally separated though. They were born together and will remain so for their lifetimes. The alien Buster finally makes it to the Atlantic ocean. He rises to the surface and feels his other self tell him that he is not going to find his ship in the Atlantic Ocean. He swims toward a shore and changes back to a human form. He then throws up. The polluted fresh water and saltwater of the ocean didn't mix well with his insides. He now knows that he can never escape his other self. He was born alien and human and now he is both of them. His human brother is still in his mind. They are Buster. Now Buster is laying on a beach somewhere on the east coast of America nude and without a clue as to how he will get to his ship.

THE BUSTERS JOIN TOGETHER TO FIND A WAY

The alien Buster gasps for breath as he crawls onto a beach somewhere on the east coast. The human Buster sends him his thoughts.

"You are not going to find what you need to find there. You must go toward the other sea."

The alien Buster now knows he is two people on this planet. He is a lost child. The human Buster is not retarded. He is just human. The two Busters are one and they now understand that they need to work as one. Buster is not a alien or a human. He is "A Top Secret baby!"

The alien Buster understands he will need his other self to survive on this planet. He opens their brain links.

"We are one! Just walking this world as two. Help me brother."

"Brother, you must go toward the west coast of this land mass and find nothing much but what this planet calls deserts. I have the mind of a very advanced human and know a lot. I will play like a retard for their government so you can get to where your ship crashed. We are one!"

"I thank you, but what do we call each other in our thoughts?"

"Buster! That is our entry word to each other's thoughts. Now find a city and say you are a lost child looking to find his way back home. You won't be lying? We are one that is two. My family wants to forget us! The government of this country wants to breed us if we can be used for their benefit. We are the unknown that they produced and know nothing about. Just find a way to go toward the west lands of this planet. I hope I am speaking in a language you can understand?"

"I will head west. I am using my species navigational skills. Am I speaking the right words?"

"Yes! Go west!"

The brothers are now one again. They just can't be together. The brothers were now connected and separated. It is a very strange relationship. Buster looks up to see a human couple run toward him. He rolls over and pretends to be cold.

BUSTER IS ON HIS WAY WEST

The couple help him stand up and wrap a coat around him. Buster pretends to shiver. They ask him all sorts of questions, so he tells them he can't remember anything. He is a mystery child now because he has no ID or any other thing that can identify him. His fingerprints are not on file because he changed them. He changed his forked tongue back to a normal looking one and now understands he really must have a purpose here on this strange planet. He is rushed to a hospital where he will be examined. He makes his form as human as he can. He opens his mind to his brother, "Buster!"

"Brother! We need to think as one from now on. I will be the one the government of this planet analyzes, you are not even a person noticed as missing. Just go west and try to find your ship."

The alien Buster changes into an old man and walks out of the hospital unnoticed. The human Buster has a nose bleed. His brother is still part of him. The alien Buster also has a nose bleed. They both need to think. They see from both their eyes. They are far apart but their minds are still connected. Both Busters need to understand that they are just one. The alien Buster must go west while the human Buster must deal with the government. It is not a healthy bond. Both of the Busters wipe their noses.They are dying.

THE HANGER

The ship that the alien crash-landed in is now in a forgotten hanger in New Mexico. The alien Buster is now an old man. He goes to a highway and decides to hitchhike his way west in hopes of picking up some sort of message from his ship. He catches a ride with a trucker who needs to tell someone his sad story about his failed marriage and life in general. Buster just lets him talk while he contemplates what he will do when he gets some sort of message from his ship. He is still half of a country away from his ship. The trucker is going to Colorado though. They make it to Denver. He leaves the trucker and turns himself into a child again. He needs to go south. His navigational skills are kicking in. He glows green and he turns into a lizard for a moment. He knows he is a alien on this planet, but he must get to his ship. He just felt the lizard thing was a clue from his ship. His human Buster was dealing with the government's questions. Both were not seeing what each of their bodies were going through. Both of their noses began bleeding again. They were not connected properly. They were still just one Buster in two different forms. They would need to become one again or both would die. Both of the Busters fall to their knees and begin to chant.

"We are one. We need to become one again. The ship must be found!"

The Buster in Virginia falls to the floor and begins foaming at the mouth.

The other Buster falls to the ground in Denver and also foams at his mouth. They would now have become one again, but at what a cost? They have to find the ship. Both Busters are foaming at the mouth and the Virginia Buster is sedated very heavily. The Buster in Colorado rolls over and lays on a cold floor. He is not dressed for the Colorado weather. His body starts to freeze. He is dying. The Buster in Virginia starts to freeze also. Doctors are there to try to make him recover. The Buster in Virginia dies. So does the Buster in Colorado. They never made it to their ship. The ship is still in a forgotten hanger in New Mexico.

AFTERMATH

Charles Franklin rushes his wife to the hospital. After the death of their son Buster they must both try to live a normal life. His wife was now again about to give birth. She goes into labor. It is a girl child. The girl child smiles into the eyes of her parents and wonders when she can find out how to get to her ship?

WRITER NOTE

Sometimes reality becomes lost in the supernatural. What if werewolves do exist? What if they are evolving or mutating as I like to say into something more than the normal werewolf? This story just might make sense if werewolves do exist. I just write! You have to digest it. There could never be sister werwolves in a pack, or could there be? Let us just imagine that there were two sister werewolves? What do werewolves eat anyway? I think their diet matters! This tale just got interesting! A story about sister werewolves just got written. Maybe we will find out what they eat?

THE SISTERS

FREDDY SMELLS THE AIR. IT stinks of female urine. The sisters used this spot to protect his territory. They are spraying the area with their piss. They are trying to hide their brother's odor. This is their way of protecting their brother. He is the alpha male in this pack but he is under attack from other packs.

The sisters are quite a change from normal werewolves. In the past most were male. Dominate sisters is very abnormal. Freddy is also abnormal. He can change into a werewolf or a human whenever he wants to. His sisters on the other hand just stand guard. They are killers and enjoy the taste of other werewolve's blood. Freddy stands and stretches. He is ready to prowl the night. He sniffs the air. He can kill without a problem. There are no other hunters in the area. He changes into his wolf persona. He runs off to find some prey.

THE SISTERS

Werewolves are only thought to become so when there was a full moon. They can become werewolves when the moon reaches several stages though. This is only important to werewolves and the territory they control. The sisters are standing guard on their brother's territory. He is hunting and they are now in charge of the pack. There has never been a pair of sisters in a pack of werewolves before. Most packs have males that control the others. Freddy's pack has two sisters that he allows to control the pack when he hunts.

They still understand that he is the alpha male. They just protect him. They are his sisters. They think that they will only breed with alpha males. So far their brother is the only one that they have met. They are not into incest. It is strange enough to have two sisters in a pack but now all the young werewolves will have to prove themselves worthy to mate with the sisters. Other packs are smelling their urine and prowling around Freddy's territory. They want to mate with the sisters. They will not find it easy to approach them though. Freddy is also a very nasty brother. He only lets his sisters see werewolves that could never lead. Still their urine is attracting other alphas that have packs. Freddy will have to let them loose someday. He just doesn't want it to be soon. He kills a deer and tears it to pieces and eats all of it. He is covered in blood and howls at the moon. He is still the alpha male in this territory. He smells other packs coming into his territory. He runs back to find his sisters. He and they will have to fight to save his territory. Packs only control what they can protect. Freddy and his sisters are going to have to make a stand. Too many other packs are sniffing his sister's piss. They are going to make them fight for his territory. Sisters are a blessing and a curse. They will fight off most males and be loyal to him, but he now knows that they will soon have to leave the pack and form their own packs. Werewolves are solitary animals for the most part and only form packs for protection. His sisters are alpha females that like to kill other werewolves and eat them. This is something never before thought of happening. Females starting their own packs just to feed themselves. Freddy doesn't really care what they eat. He just wants them to leave his pack when it is their time. They are getting too powerful for him to control much longer. He runs back to them though and rubs up to them with the bloody fur that he is wearing. The deer's blood makes them lick him and clean the blood off of him. He is still the alpha male and his sisters are still loyal to him. He howls at the moon again. He just doesn't know how much longer his sisters will follow him. Freddy is not the first werewolf to wonder what would happen if female werewolves want to be alphas. He cares little about the past, he is not worried about the future either. His sisters could very easily become the future though. They kill and eat other werewolves. For now though he is the most powerful male werewolf out there because he has two sisters who fight with him. He sniffs the air. His rivals are coming. He knows that they can not defeat him. He is still the alpha male and has his two sisters so he can fight from three different sides. Besides the other packs won't join together because they too must defend their territories. For now they are the three alphas all other werewolves must fear. When it is time for them to split up is what he doesn't want to foresee. He falls into a state of sleep that he needs. His sisters guard his resting place. Freddy awakes to find no pack was willing to attack his territory He is now reaching an age that werewolves fear. He is now going to have to reproduce and his sisters will reach this age soon. He fears for his pack and knows that it is just nature taking control. All creatures must find a way to continue. His time is now coming. He looks up at the full moon and howls. He will soon have to take the path toward separation from his sisters and mate. He howls again. No wolf or werewolf can not hear these howls. He is going to become a lone alpha wolf soon. The sisters will have to be banished from his pack because Freddy has to mate. His sisters will have to do so soon after. Freddy must banish the sisters before he mates. His pack is safe with three alphas, but all three will need to form their own packs in order to mate. It is now the time to form three packs that can control the others. But can Freddy rule alone? That is now the question his pack is wondering. They have been under Freddy and his two sisters rule for so many years that change frightens them. Freddy turns into his werewolf self and howls at the moon for maybe his last time as the alpha male controlling his sisters. He howls again asking the moon what can he do? But there is no way the moon can let him keep his sisters next to him. They must breed more werewolves from his bloodline. He must make at least one male offspring. He howls again and smells the other packs coming in for the kill. Tonight he and his sisters must fight off other packs. He again turns into his werewolf self and motions for his sisters to join him. Tonight might be their last time fighting together as a pack. He runs and all his pack follows. He and his sisters will fight tonight. It will be another victory he guesses. The other packs don't have a male brother and two sisters to lead them. They all howl at the moon and run toward a slaughter. Freddy feels that this will be his last battle with his sisters. He must mate and they will be banished. He will probably have to fight one or the other of their packs in the future. That is the fate of werewolves. They all have to become solitary animals sometime in their lives. Freddy leads his sisters into a battle that he thinks will break his family up. What was once a family will soon become three families. He knows he must let his sisters go but he will lead them to one more victory. He howls his leader howl and his sisters and his pack attack the invading werewolves. They fight fiercely to protect his territory. Wolves howl in the forests around the fight. They smell the blood. Freddy smells victory and defeat. He will lose his sisters this night. Three packs will emerge from this last stand. After the battle Freddy howls at the moon and releases his sisters to form their own packs. They trot off into the forest and they separate. Freddy takes a pretty werewolf as his wife. The sisters turn into their human forms and head for villages where they can make their followers. One goes east and the other west. The sisters are now lone wolves. They have until the next full moon to make their territories.

THREE YEARS LATER

Melissa is the oldest of the sisters. She mated and killed her mate, but she was impregnated and bore a male child. She and her pack are now mercenaries. They kill only for money. She lets her son count the bounties that her pack collects. She is not afraid of Freddy's pack.

She is his sister and she stays away from his territory. She knows her brother and how bad he is. She smells him in her dreams. He has something that make the sisters want to protect him still. She still wants to protect him even after forming her own pack. She has her own pack now and a male alpha child that is growing up. She still kills any male that thinks it is an alpha in her pack and eats him. Her taste for werewolf meat is still strong. Her son will follow her in ruling her pack. Still, Freddy is the alpha male she will always protect. A alpha female werewolf is a rarity but these two sisters are going to change the species forever. They are Freddy's sisters and fought and killed along side him while they were young. He will always be their big brother and a leader of the pack. Melissa turns into her wolf self and howls at the full moon. She wonders about her sister and brother. She wants to know them again.

Bethany is the youngest sister. She mated with a very strange werewolf. He is nothing like her brother. Her brother kills and asked his sisters to kill with him. They ruled his territory with bloodlust. Her brother was bad and ruled his pack as if he owned the planet. He killed and enjoyed it. He taught his pack to kill for pleasure. His sisters were his best pupils. Now three years separated her from Freddy but she still wants to protect him. Bethany has a werewolf mate that is docile. He only kills when he needs to feed. She still kills for pleasure. She wants him to be Freddy, but Freddy is her brother and her teacher. Micky is just a werewolf that fucks her. She still hasn't born a male alpha. She misses Freddy and Melissa. She turns into her wolf self and howls at the moon. She wants to join Freddy in a kill with Melissa. She misses the slaughter they produced when they ruled the pack. She was the female Freddy. "Baby sister" the one Freddy always let kill first. He watched her as she killed without guilt. He understood that she was special in her kills. She was so like him, yet she was not him. She could rule a pack that would rival Freddy's pack someday.

FREDDY

Freddy smelled his sisters still. Bethany was the sister he feared the most. He was still an alpha male werewolf and had a territory to protect. Bethany had a pack that didn't understand the way the brother and two sisters killed. Bethany was still learning what a sister werewolf was. Freddy had a three year old. He was the next Freddy if he lived long enough. He didn't know Bethany was still without a male offspring. She fucks but can not get pregnant. She loves her husband but feels he is incapable of getting her pregnant. She decides it is time to kill him and his family. She sends her most trusted werewolves to complete the kill. She is now a widow werewolf. Maybe the first of her kind. She knows that she and Freddy will have to meet again to make some sort of treaty. She is a nasty bitch and she thinks that she is the female Freddy. She just killed her husband and his family and only smiles. She eats her husband and shares the rest of his family with her pack. She is going to try to reunite with her big brother and sister. She wants the past to become the future. She leads her pack into the woods and follows Freddy's scent. She turns into her wolf persona and howls. She is bringing her pack into Freddy's territory. Melissa hears the howl and moves her pack toward Freddy's. The family will either own the night or die trying. The sisters want to kill again with their brother. Freddy just must let them return to his pack. He smells his sisters entering into his territory. He howls for his pack to take a defensive position. His sister's packs are at least equal to his pack. He has fought beside them and decides it is time for a family reunion. He becomes human and walks toward his sisters. They also turn human. They sniff each other and then hug. Freddy will allow his sisters to hunt with him again. They are family. The three packs join as one. Freddy turns into his wolf persona and runs into the forest to kill. Melissa and Bethany meet Freddy's child and lick him. Freddy's child licks Melissa's boy. They have met. Freddy is killing something and the sisters now take control of the three packs. They have come back to a family pack. Freddy howls at the moon as he seeks his next kill. His sisters protect his territory. Family is what matters. The sisters and Freddy's and Melissa's children take control of the the three packs. They all howl at a full moon and change into werewolves. Freddy is special and his sisters just want to be part of his pack. They let him hunt and control the packs like in the past. Freddy will always be the alpha male in their family. Bethany kills an alpha male just for food. She is still barren but she wants to breed the next Freddy. She is a bitch in heat. Freddy is just happy to have his sisters back in his pack. I repeat! Family is what matters! Welcome back to the pack!

writer's note:

There are ships flying around in space and some of the inhabitants in these vessels are wondering where they are heading because supplies are not arriving on a normal schedule and that is causing them to contact the SpaceTesting Ground with complaints. Sara is their main contact and she just received a message from one of the first and farthest away satellites. It's occupant is freaking out. The message is loud and clear. She records it and will rush it to her superiors.

"I am eating my hair. I just shaved the rest of my body. I only have what is left of my hair on a plate in front of me. I need supplies soon or I will have to start eating parts of my body. I am not insane because there is no sanity in outer space. Please save me!"

SPACE FARE 2

THEY ARE STILL OUT THERE

SARA HEARS THE WORDS BUT can't believe what she is hearing. The rejected people of the past are now trying to understand why they were doomed to live in outer space and now their supplies are not coming. The ships are all on the same radio frequency. They are now talking among themselves and have decided to turn around their ships and head back to earth. They are tired of being in space with no destination and having to start eating their own hair because supplies have stopped arriving. They now want revenge. These were the most prolific killers on the planet and were doomed to what earth thought was a prison in outer space. Now they are turning their ships around and returning to earth. Sara can no longer lie to them. She runs to her superior's office.

She speaks with terror in her voice. "They are coming home."

LIFE IS SHORT

Sara gives the news to the people that control the Space Testing Agency. The criminals are now coming home. Earth is now pretty stable and there is no crime. Bringing criminals back to the planet is not what anyone wants. The criminals don't care. They actually control their ships. They can bring them back to earth. They are starving and that makes a criminal want to kill. They are coming home to kill. They have spent enough time in space. They now want a place on earth. They were the world's best killers in their time and now they will create a new version of outlaw! They all press a key that sends a message to Sara from all of them into the computer that lets them keep in contact with the Space Testing Center and Sara.

"We are coming home and want revenge."

The computer replies that the new coordinates would be programed into their ships. They will be coming back to earth and the computers at the Space Testing Ground had allowed for this. Earth will now receive back the most dangerous people it wanted to forget. Life is short. People that were forgotten now want to be known. Space was just a prison that contained them from society. It can not keep the unwanted from returning. It was just a prison in space. Now they are bringing back what these criminals have learned from years in space. It is anyone's guess what? They only talked to a person by the name of Sara for many years circling the world that discarded them like garbage.

Sara looks her superior in his eyes and realizes she will die unless she can talk him into letting her talk to these criminals.

"They talk to me. Let me talk to them."

"It is too late!"

Sara understands that the people she talked to in outer space will be killed. They no longer matter. She was hoping she did?

SARA

Sara has been in contact with the planet's last professional killers for way too many years. These killers were sent into space to rid the world of their kind. They were sent into space because the planet didn't know what to do with them. They still were alive and capable of remembering their trade. Now they were returning and Sara wasn't sure anyone could control them. Sara was scared. Sara would have to try and talk them out of returning to earth. She knew that this was not going to happen. Killers were just that. They were coming home and had a grudge. They wanted revenge. Sara was their only voice on the planet that had discarded them like garbage so many many years ago. They had been sent into space for so many years and no one really gave a shit about them. They now were not receiving supplies and that pissed them off. Now Sara had to speak to them or at least she hoped she could.

"You are not welcome on earth. Please don't come back. The authorities will kill you. I am trying to save your lives." She was begging to them.

Max then spoke to Sara.

"I have been eating my hair. If you think I want to play nice then you sent the wrong man into outer space."

Sara gripped the computer keyboard like a vice.

"Let them kill us! We have nothing left. I for one want my old life back."

Max signed off. Sara tried every way she could to reconnect to Max.

He was coming back to the Space Testing Ground with the other discards. Sara could not save them or her. Everyone involved in the disposal of people by sending them into space failed. Sara walked down the hallway toward her superiors. She was not going to walk back from that hallway. Space had won. Testing it had failed. Sara spoke to her superiors.

"We failed! They are coming home!"

Sara cut her throat. She knew that nothing was going to stop them from returning.

The Space Testing Ground programed the ships it sent into space to return. Now they were. What was returning was not what they sent into space. The earth was in for a surprise. Sara was just the first to die.

The first ship landed on the Space Testing Ground's landing field.

Max stepped out of his ship!

"I am back!"

He shouted it so anyone that was in hearing distance would hear him. He was shaved bald and had no hair anywhere else on his body. He had eyes that wanted revenge. Two more ships landed. They were the other two who their countries sent to be exiled in outer space. They were a team now. They now had something in common. They were the best killers while on earth and now they had come back to become the worst killers outer space could create. The Space Center sent armed personnel to kill them. Max was the first to die. Earth killed them. They were not welcome in the new world. Outer space needed to remain a place that no one came back from. The other two outcasts were shot and killed.The deaths that happened this day made sure that no one comes home from outer space. The space center was readying three more rockets it was planning to launch. Space was just a prison no one came back from.

Writer's note.

This story is an introduction into another world. It is about a man who has killed and has remorse. He lines up seven guns on a table in front of him. He has used all but one of them in his profession. He kills people for a living. He is saving the seventh gun for his final act on this planet. His death. He doesn't know that the final gun was given to him by a witch. He is about to find out about the seventh gun and it's bullet

second writer's note:

This story is very disturbing because it deals with life after death. What if you awoke on a stainless steel table in a morgue and you didn't know why? The only answer to the questions flowing through your mind should be why am I wearing a toe tag if I am still alive? A very disturbing story but a good read. Just trust me! This is a tale that will keep your toe tapping!

TOE TAG

Lawrence awakes on a stainless steel table. He remembers shooting a bullet into his brain. He should be dead. He isn't though. The table is cold and he shivers. His mind is now awake and he is wondering why he is still alive? He is sure there will be other people thinking the same. He shot himself with a bullet in a gun that he was given in a coffee shop by a woman he could only remember as if she was just a blur. He just didn't know the seventh gun and single bullet was not for him to kill himself with. He now needs to find out why he is still alive! He removes the toe tag from his foot and stands up in the morgue. He is nude. He needs to find some clothes and a reason why he is not dead. He rummages through the lockers and finds sealed evidence clothing in sealed bags. He tears them open until he finds some clothing that make him look more than a homeless person. The clothes stink of death. He walks toward a door that will lead him out of the morgue. He wasn't autopsied so he was still a whole person. He finds the door that will lead him out of the morgue. He is living a nightmare. He smells like he hasn't bathed in days and he runs into the night as if he was knowing where he was going. He stops in the middle of a road and has to jump to the curb before being run over. He doesn't even know where he is. He grabs his head to try to remember the last thing he saw before pulling the trigger on the gun that was supposed to kill him. All he can see is empty pages. He just wanted to end his life. He rubs his eyes. He is all alone and has no memory. He is also wearing dead people's clothing and has no money. He is pretty much screwed and up the river without a paddle. He sits down on the curb and smiles. He looks at his feet. He is wearing one black sneaker and a white one. He laughs out loud. He used to be a killer is all he can recollect. He now remembers that the seventh gun and it's bullet were a gift. The person that gave it to him was a person that he only met once. He remembered that she looked like she was in a fog. He remembered watching her leave and turn and blow him a kiss. The gun and a single bullet were in front of him on a table in a coffee shop. She just disappeared before he could say anything. He really never knew why he saved the gun and the bullet. He just knew that now they had made him the walking dead or worse. He spit and stood up. He was not dead or at least his body wasn't. He felt his head to find the bullet wound that should have killed him. It wasn't there. Either he was insane or something abnormal was happening to him. He now was homeless and smelled bad. He was wearing dead people's clothes that didn't even match. He needed to find someone that could help him. His mind raced! He remembered a bank that he had hidden some of his payments from his kills. He was thinking that there were more. Lawrence was now alive and now had to find a way to understand how he was standing on a street corner after shooting himself in his head. He just needed to remember the bank and how to get the money out. He stood up and walked toward he was not sure where. He seemed to know the way though. That was what he couldn't understand. He needed to find the woman. The one who gave him the gun and the bullet. He walked into a bank and after many questions because he had no ID, he withdrew four thousand dollars. He would now look for the woman that gave him a gun and a bullet. The problem was she was in a fog when he met her. He never thought about how odd it was that she just showed up at a coffee shop he was in and left a gun and a bullet. He was on a job at the time. He just took them and hid them in his clothes. He saved them though. That was the problem. He kept them and tried to end his life with them. It didn't happen. Now he needed to know why? He walked out of the bank with no clue as to where he was going. He was looking for a mystery woman. She was definitely a mystery to him. He just walked around confused and not sure where he would end up. He sat down on a street corner wondering if he was ever going to understand what had happened to him. He wept. He was totally lost! He took off the mismatched sneakers and threw them into the oncoming traffic.

He then stood up and went to a hotel that he didn't remember that he had been there before.

"Welcome back Mr Lloyd."

The Porter knew him. He just walked past him and went to the front desk.

"Mr Lloyd it has been a while."

He stared at the desk clerk like she was something out of book he was reading.

Lawrence just didn't know what was happening to him.

"My regular room and someone that can get me some new clothes."

"As you wish."

The clerk gave him a key card to room 666. He took it and headed for the elevator. He didn't know how or why he was in this hotel, but it might give him some clue as to who he was. He hoped so. Lawrence was going to find out that there was life after death. He used the only gun that couldn't kill him with the only bullet that could make him understand that he was special. He would now face his past. Most people never got this special treatment. Lawrence would now find out who he was. He had been given a gun and a bullet that would change his life forever. Lawrence was about to relive his past. The witch that gave him the gun and the bullet entered the hotel and went to the elevator. She pressed the button that would take her to room 666. Lawrence turned the shower to hot. He was going to wash himself. He just didn't know who would walk out of the shower. He never thought he would meet the witch that brought him there. She held a towel for him. He just walked around her. He was now not alive. He died and was resurrected on a table in a morgue. He was now facing a person that he absolutely needed to meet. She smiled at him. She blew him a kiss. She had done so once before. Now he was going to try and remember that moment. A moment in a coffee shop. He accepted her kiss. He just wished he had saved the toe tag so he could throw it in her face. He only remembered a moment that he never thought he would remember. She just blew him another kiss. He would now pay for his sins. She walked toward the door to the hotel room and turned toward him.

"You will find Hell! You are just beginning your journey!"

She closed the hotel room door.

Lawrence knew he was fucked. The woman that gave him the gun wanted more than his soul. He guessed she wanted him to pay for the souls he had killed.

He fell to his knees and sputtered these words.

"I am not a person that can be forgiven."

He was about to face his maker. He just didn't know who his maker was?

He was about to find out though.

The woman he needed answers from just shut the door on him.

He opened the door to his hotel room and fell to his knees. He saw her standing in front of the elevator.

"I just want you to understand me."

She shrugged her head and entered the elevator.

"I gave you a choice once and you tried to kill yourself with it. You are on your own from now on."

The elevator door closed.

Lawrence now figured out that he was going to see his life unfold before him. He couldn't die until he understood why he was who he had become.

THE MORGUE

Lawrence went back into the room and closed the door. On the coffee table was the same gun and a bullet. He fumbled toward the coffee table and loaded the gun with the one bullet. He held it to his head and pulled the trigger. The gunshot sound was loud and clear.

Lawrence held the gun in his hands just looking at it. He had failed again to kill himself with the gun and the bullet. Lawrence was now laying on a stainless steel table in a morgue. Lawrence screamed. He looked down at his feet. He wore a toe tag. He was dying all over again

WRITER NOTE

Rednecks are everywhere. They are even in other countries. Sometimes though a special one shows up. This story is about one that never should have been born. He is the worst redneck you would never want to meet. Welcome to his world! He has arrived on television and the internet via late night cable. Read his story. I am trying to write it without puking! He even makes me feel like there has to be a stopping point when we deal with rednecks! I just puked! Sambo wants his day in court! I just want to puke again. I just did!

SAMBO JENKINS

LATE NIGHT SATURDAY ON CABLE television. A program is being televised in a garage in Houston, Texas. A guy by the name of Sambo Jenkins is being televised on a show filmed in a garage.

"Hey ya all! I am white but my name sounds like I am a nigger."

He drinks from a bottle of tequila and falls face down on a concrete driveway.

He somehow manages to get upright. He stares at the camera.

"I am still alive. I think that my life is a horror story."

He walks over to the camera and kisses it.

"I am fucked up!"

He turns away from the camera and pisses on the driveway.

"Opps! I just couldn't help myself. I'm a fuck up and people are filming it."

He looks at the camera and then falls face first on the pavement. He tries to stand up but just fumbles around with no way of getting on his feet. He finally just falls down and smiles up at the camera.

"Welcome to my garage."

He takes another drink of tequila.

"I drink this Spic shit booze because it is cheap and I live in Texas.

He fumbles around the driveway and John is having a hard time keeping him on camera.

"I'm a redneck mother fucker. I don't work because I drink too much and people don't like it when they smell my breath. I usually beg for money on street corners and people pay me to leave them alone. I live in a garage because this house is for sale and I can sneak in at night without anyone knowing I am here."

He falls down again. He stands up and moons John. He is bleeding from the pavement meeting his face.

"I'm Sambo Jenkins. I just don't want to be anyone. I just want to get fucked up and shoot the finger at everyone. Do you see this?"

He shoots his middle finger at the camera and stumbles around trying to stay on his feet. He still falls down and John makes sure he gets the full face to the pavement shot. John Wilson is hoping the American public will buy into a redneck that is on a suicidal trip. He films Sambo throwing up. Sambo still can shoot the finger at the camera. though.

"Fuck you! I don't give a shit!"

His face is a mess and is bleeding. John rushes toward him and covers his face with towels. Sambo gave a good performance. John sits down and covers his eyes. Sambo is going to either make or break him. Right now he has to move him. He lifts the bleeding Sambo up and takes him into the garage and lays him down on sheets he brought for just such a occasion. He looks down at Sambo and hopes he will live through the night. He takes his camera to his van and studies the shots he took this night.

TOMORROW

Sambo is still sleeping in a garage in a house up for sale. John Wilson is in debt and only can afford film for his camera by writing bad checks. Sambo Jenkins is his only hope of becoming a functioning person in this world. He will get a deal to show the films of this sorry redneck on late night cable if he catches his death on film. He will fulfill his contact and will be given four hundred dollars. He buys more film. Sambo is going to make him famous or at least that is what he thinks. Sambo is Sambo after all and there are just so many houses that are up for sale in Houston. He lifts Sambo up from the garage floor and wraps him in the sheets he was laying on and puts him in the back seat of a toyota van. He drives off in a huff. This guy is not going to live much longer. He needs for him to last for a while so some late night cable shows that cater to the drunk twenty somethings will watch and he can collect a regular paycheck. Sambo is just a show he must provide or he will lose everything. He drives fast and stops at a house that is for sale. He knows that no one will show up until the weekend. He pulls Sambo from the car and gives him a bottle of tiquila. He speaks into his ear.

"Get on your feet. He turns his camera on. He needs more film.

Sambo moons the camera. He is so fucked up on tiquila that he falls down hard on the driveway. He turns toward the camera and slurs at it.

"I just shit in my pants."

TOMORROW AGAIN

John strips Jasper from his clothes holding his nose. He has to make this show tonight. Jasper is so drunk he doesn't know he is being stripped. John is hoping there is a water outlet at this house. He has a hose in his van. He has had to use it too many times. He finds one and attaches the the hose. He sprays Sambo down and then goes toward his clothes. They smell really bad. He only has so many hours before he has to film Jasper being Jasper. He gives him another bottle of tiquila as he washes his clothes to get rid of the shit Jasper couldn't hold in. John loads his camera and looks at Jasper. He is dying. He would feel sorry for him but he needs to film his death, if it will happen, on late night cable. Jasper is the redneck no one wants to meet. He just doesn't give a shit and tells everyone who will listen that this is so. Jasper finishes off the bottle and screams at John.

"Give me another bottle or I will fart till no one can come within ten feet of me!"

John asks Sambo to repeat his threat. He is filming him now.

Sambo repeats his threat. John is happy. He has his shows opening moment. Jasper is ready to perform. He gives him another bottle. Jasper fumbles around the driveway, nude, and definitely drunk. John keeps filming him.

SAMBO COMES CLEAN

"Niggers, spics, jews and the rest of you mother fucking assholes. I eat your fucking manufactured food and crap daily. You just don't understand. I just can't like you. I want to become the swamp that you don't want to find. Jasper moons the camera. John is feeling good. The late night crowd will love the moon that Jasper just produced. He checks to see how much film he has left. He turns off his camera.

John just wants to see Jasper die on camera. Jasper just wants another drink. Maybe there is still a show! John just needs for Jasper to live a few more days. John turns from the camera and calls his contact at a local news station. Jasper has to die on camera he is told. John hopes he can film it!

John walks back to where he left Jasper. Jasper is lying on the driveway with puke flowing from his mouth. He is dead. John just found out he should probably join him. He missed the final shot that he needed. Jasper just made John unemployed.

John filmed Jasper's dying body anyways. He hoped it would be enough for him to get someone to buy him film for his next project!

Book Two

"WAG A TALE"

*I thought writing stories were cool until
I discovered tales. Just read on*

Writer's note:
*What if you could tell people's futures? I am not saying that a person really
can see a person's future, I am just saying what if a person could convince
people that he could? This is a tale of one such a man. He just guesses about
what people want to hear and asks them to pay him to tell them what they
should do. He is good at it! Most people become what he tells them they will
become. He is "The Fortune Teller." The trouble is he didn't see his future.
Now he will see the only future that matters. "His!"*

FORTUNE TELLER

FRANK WAS JUST A REGULAR guy struggling to make a living. He was sitting in a bar one night and a man asked him to read his fortune by looking at his hand. The guy was drunk and Hank was trying to get there. He told the guy he would become a real estate agent. The guy gave him a hundred dollar bill. The guy became a real estate agent. Hank became a fortune teller that night. He made someone think they could become what he predicted. After that night he just became "The Fortune Teller." He kept going to bars to find fools that would pay him to read their fortunes by looking at their hands. Most of them became what he predicted. He was making a nice living telling drunk people what they wanted to hear. They told their friends about him and he became a person most people wanted to meet. He really had become "The Fortune Teller." He was just a guy that told people what they wanted to hear. He was just a guy you met in a bar that listened to you while you told him your hopes and dreams while intoxicated. Maybe he really was a fortune teller? He had a good record of making people become what they wanted to be. He just met people that were desperate and intoxicated. He was very good at predicting futures when these people were intoxicated. He was not very good with sober people though. Sober people were too hard to lie to and they wouldn't spill out their pathetic lives to him. He was always about the lie. He was not going to tell anyone they were just stupid fools looking for a reason to change into somebody they would probably become anyway. He just took their money and told them they had a future. Most of them did find that future though. That was what made him such a success. Frank sat on a barstool in Washington DC. He was drunk and about to meet *the last person he ever thought he would meet. She was a person that had no fortune to read. She had one to tell. His!. She was his wake up call. She was going to become Frank's last fortune to predict. His! She sat down next to him and ran her fingers over his dick. He stared at her and fell in love. He was now just a dick on a barstool next to one of the most attractive women he had ever met. He never saw her coming. He was about to read his fortune. It was not what he was expecting. She whispered into his ear. "You are now going to see your fortune and it will not be what you expected."*

He has a erection.

She rubs his erection. He ejaculates into his pants.

She whispers into his ear again."You will do what I say."

Frank was now just a fool sitting on a barstool with cum in his pants. The woman next to him had just made him her slave. He slobbered out the words, "What do you want me to predict?"

She spoke quietly but loud enough for Frank to hear her.

"You are now my fortune teller. I will need you to control certain people that are in power."

Frank just slobbered some more. This witch or whatever she was had taken control of his mind.

Frank just became a "Fortune Teller" for a beautiful witch in Washington DC and that is the reason we don't need politicians? Witches are better at the game than they are. Frank was led out of the bar by his witch so he could wash up and change his pants and underwear. His new witch needed him to tell some fortunes.

A ELECTION YEAR

Frank changed while the lady he met in the bar looked around his kitchen. She was looking for spices and other ingredients that could make his life more than just meat and potatoes. Frank was no chef. His kitchen was pathetic. She was now not sure Frank was the guy she needed to tell the fortunes of the people she needed him to meet. She slammed the door on a cabinet that should have been filled with spices. She looked at Frank and screamed at him."We are going shopping!"

Frank now cleaned up, was just her tool. He followed her out of his apartment and they headed for "Trader Joe's." She needed to reinvent him for his next act as "Fortune Teller." Frank was going to learn how to cook so he could enjoy the life that his new master needed him to fit into.

She spoke. "My name is, let us just say, Paula."

She began throwing spices in a shopping cart. She needed to work fast. It was a election year and they had a lot of shopping to do.

Bitch of a witch

Washington DC is a cesspool. Money is easily available and those who control it are no more than rats feeding on the best garbage available. Frank looks into Paula's eyes and his head starts to lose it's memories. His mind is now just a pad of paper that needs to be filled. Paula is about to start on page one. She takes him back to his apartment and throws a ribeye in a frying pan. He was now going to learn how to cook for the big guys and gals in DC. At least that is what she hopes. Most politicians are alcoholics. Frank seems to know how to make them believe in a fortune teller. She takes the spices out of her shopping bag and makes a ribeye that most politicians would die for. Frank just watches as she flips the steak over. He is bewitched! Now Paula will lead him toward a new government.

POLITICS

Now Frank knows drunks. He is in heaven in Washington DC. His new girl or witch or whatever is having him look for big game. It won't be long before he finds them. Washington DC is full of drunken politicians. Frank enters a bar where most of Congress buries their next victims. He finds a barstool far from the center and watches his marks come in. He is sitting next to the woman he will never be able to describe to anyone in his future.

She just needs him to tell fortunes to some very special people. She speaks into his ear. "You will just suggest that there will be a war to end all wars!

FRANK

Frank walks over and spills his drink on Senator Perkins, the highest ranked senator for the Republicans.

"I am so sorry. Can I refresh your drink?"

He had his introduction. His witch or whatever just smiles at him. He is on fire. He sits down next to the senator and asks if he wants his fortune read. Frank is really going to tell fortunes of the few people that really needed their fortunes told. He smiles at the senator as the lady he came in with left the bar. Frank was now on his own. He would only tell fortunes for politicians! Yeah! If only this tale was real?

Writer's note:

What if you woke up beside a woman that was tattooed from her neck to her ankles? She wasn't beautiful unless you consider ink injected into a body as a form of art. Her body was supple and she had decent breasts and a very nice ass but what made her special was her tattoos. She had so many stories on her body that no one man could ever try to read them all. Each tattoo had a story attached to it though. She was "The Tattooed Lady!" This tale is very cool. She makes this guy want to read them all. She also makes me want to tell the stories committed to ink on everybody's body. Anybody else interested?

THE TATTOOED LADY

PAUL WOKE UP BESIDE A *tattooed woman. He didn't remember how he got to where he was now. Paul was in his bed with a tattooed lady though and neither of them were wearing any clothes. She rolled over and kissed him deeply. She asked him if he wanted to have sex with her again? We just did it he guessed? He had no memory of what happened the last few minutes of his life. She then asked him to make her a cup of coffee. He brought her the cup but she jumped him again. He wanted to tattoo her with something of his making but he just fucked her. It was all he could do. This girl had been around. Paul was not sure if he was safe in her presence. Her body had more stories on it than most writers could produce in their lifetime. Paul was a writer. He looked at her tattoos and hoped to find a story about why she had to paint her body with tattoos? She just fucked him again. He just wanted her to let him see her tattoos. She told him he would have to fuck her for each one she told him about. She was the tattooed lady. He was young, well hung, and ready to try. She told him to look at the one on her right breast. It was only what he could describe as a pirate.*

"He was the best pirate I ever met."

Paul wanted to know about the pirate. He kissed the tit and then passed out. She was making him want to read her whole body. He was hooked. She was the "Tattooed Lady."

When he awoke she was above him staring down at him. She laughed very sexy,

"You have two tattoos that need to be read. You fucked me for them. One is for the pirate's story."

"You didn't let me ask you about the pirate was all Paul could spit out of his mouth as she mounted him."

Paul was not fully awake yet but understood she was going to tell him the story of the pirate. Paul just smiled at her and said, "I am your slave. Tell me the story."

Paul as a writer needs all sorts of inspiration to come up with story lines. This girl's body was filled with them and he was just on number one. Paul just hoped his dick could handle the use it was about to get. Paul just looked up at the tattoos. He couldn't even see her anymore. She was just a bunch of tattoos that needed to be read.

She spoke. "The pirate was the best pirate in the new world. I am talking the modern world. He lived in Miami but traveled the caribbean with no fear of the authorities. He smuggled drugs, guns, women, and even antiquities. He just was the best pirate out there. I met him in Miami while I was just 14. He looked so magnificent that I just fucked him. I got my right breast tattooed the next day. Unfortunately for him that was his last day on earth. The DEA shot him with so many bullets he wasn't available for a open casket. He never got to see his tattoo."

Now you owe me a fuck. She mounted Paul and somehow he arose to the occasion.

Paul then went to his computer and wrote a short story entitled "The Pirate."

The pages just kept flowing and before he knew it he had a thirty two page short story.

He then went back to his bed and spoke to the tattooed person laying on it waiting for him.

"I just gave you a free fuck because you never gave me another tattoo to read."

She laughed hard and long.

She pulled him down on the soiled sheets and spoke into his ear. "You are going to be two tattoos behind. Come here."

STORIES FOR TATTOOS

Paul sighed and fucked his tattooed lady. He wanted more stories. She showed him her left breast. It was a dog! Paul gasped. A dog was something different. She just smiled and told him he would have to fuck her to get another story! Paul somehow arose to the occasion. He was now going to read "The Dog!"

The dog was a german shepherd. It was supposed to be a guard dog. It was just a lap dog to her, but very protective. The lady of the house had many secrets she kept from her husband. One of them was her body guard. She fucked him every chance she got. She was a very horny woman. My tattooed lady was fucking the husband and she knew it was only a matter of time before the fucking turned into real life. The rich mother fucker killed his other wife because he knew she was fucking the staff. The dog was just an innocent bystander. The husband always left the house with the tattooed lady after locking the dog out of the house. The tattooed lady turned him in to the police. Thus "The dog!" He was a witness. The dog would never let the husband near his wife. That is why he was always locked out of the house when they were together. The body guard told the police that the husband put her guard dog outside and locked doors so he could kill her. It made sense to the authorities. The dog became a tattoo.

Paul was now hooked line and sinker. She showed him her belly. It was a picture of a man screaming!

Paul just looked her in her eyes and spoke.

"What am I about to see?"

She said "Fuck me and you will find out."

Placing ink under skin to make a tattoo was just something that the world accepted. Paul was dealing with a woman that these tattoos meant something more. Every tattoo was a story and Paul was reading her. He was hooked. He just wanted to know why the man was screaming! Call him a fool or worse. Paul just needed to know this next story! He thought he was going to write a best seller! He went to his computer and wrote the dog's story.

THE SCREAMING MAN

Paul liked good whiskey and young women. He just didn't know what kind of a women he would find when he met the tattooed lady? She had a tattoo on her stomach of a screaming man. He had read two and now was hooked. Wouldn't you eat the forbidden fruit if was offered to you?

Paul was married and often cheated on his wife, that is, until he met the tattooed lady. She made him confess that he was just a fool and a very good lover!

They made love again. She panted at Paul. "This tattoo was created just for you!"

Paul lifted his head from her pussy and squeaked out a "What do you mean?"

She just laughed out loud and said "you are the screaming man."

Paul arose from the bed and ran screaming from the room totally nude. He was the screaming man.

Paul went to his computer and wrote on. This tattooed lady was really making him write. She then walked over to him and showed him her right buttox. It was not tattooed. She then showed him her left one. It was Paul in a coffin.

"We had our fun and you were a good fuck, but, a tattoo is just a tattoo unless someone reads it. You have read too many. Now I need to find my next reader."

Paul gasped for his breath but couldn't get any. He would become the last tattoo he would ever read on her. He was now just another story that would be printed in ink on the tattooed lady. She had put a poison in her pussy that was draining his strength and making his mind go blank. She sat on him staring down at his dying face and then bent down and kissed him deeply.

"I am in need of another story and my right buttox is bare."

She dismounted him and took all the money out of his wallet and left the room turning off his computer. She had a new story to write. She was a much better writer than Paul.

Writer's note:

There have been so many westerns written that they are copied over and over by the movie industry. Here is one no one ever saw or read before. The characters are very raw so those who are not ready for how the west really was should probably go to my next tale. I am going to tell a tale about how the west was before it was tamed. I am going to write "PEACE." This is a tale Larry never wrote about!

PEACE

BILL WAS JUST BILL TO *anyone who wanted to know him. He just wasn't a nice man. He turned and shot a porter! He just walked into the room at the wrong time. Bill has enemies. Bill also has a fast trigger finger. That is why he is still alive. Bill is just a cowboy on his way to Hell. The porter would just be another nobody that anyone would never miss. Bill put his gun in it's holster and smiled. He stood up, picked up his saddle bag and walked out of the hotel room. He did keep his hand on his gun though. He was not sure that there was not someone else who wanted him dead waiting around a corner. The porter was just a person that met Bill's gun! He headed for the first bar he could find. Killing always made him thirsty. He entered "The Last Resort!" This place was meant for him to enter. He still kept his hand on his gun. He pulled it out and reloaded it. He might need all the bullets in his gun. He motioned for the bartender to come over.*

"Give me two fingers of your best scotch."

He turned and shot a man entering the bar. He fired twice just to make sure the man was dead. He was a lawman. Bill didn't care. He was carrying a gun and was ready to use it. So was Bill, only he didn't hesitate when he killed someone. He drank his scotch and winked at the bartender.

"He will pay for it."

Bill held his gun over his head and stepped over the dead man and walked out of the bar. Bill was a killer. He headed for another bar. He wasn't drunk enough yet and killing made him thirsty.

Bill entered a hotel and went to the bar. He pulled his gun out and added two new bullets. He wasn't sure if he would need them but was not ready to second guess his future. He sat down facing the door to the bar. He had just killed another person and was not sure that someone might come in the door looking for revenge. He was wearing out his welcome in this town. If he killed another person then he would have to move on. He motioned for the bartender to come over to him.

"A double scotch of your best."

He then pulled out his gun and revolved the chamber. It sounded like a safe being opened. He smiled and spit on the floor. He was a killer. Bill didn't like to be surprised. The bartender brought him his scotch and hurried back to the end of the bar. Bill was just somebody you never wanted to meet.

Bill just stared at the door that was the entrance to the bar. He drew his gun. He knew someone was coming to try to kill him. He was ready for him. He revolved his gun's chambers and cocked it. He fired twice. Bill just smiled at the dead man as he hit the floor. The man fell down before Bill could even finish his drink. He reloaded his gun and finished his drink. He told the bartender that the dead man would pay for his drink. He walked out of the hotel stepping over the dead man and went looking for another bar. He just killed his second lawman and didn't really feel sorry for them. That was just the way the west was. Somebody always died. Bill just didn't want to be that somebody. That was why he became a killer! He just wanted to be the one that didn't' die. Bill found a new bar. He still faced the door and kept his hand on his gun. He ordered another double scotch from the bartender. The bartender brought it over and Bill drank it with the hand that was not on his gun. Bill knew he would kill again this day. He smiled and watched the door that entered the bar. He was about to kill again. That was the way of the west.

He ordered another double scotch.

Bill really was just the guy you didn't want to meet or ever come in contact with. His trigger finger was very fast and he killed without even thinking twice. He drew his gun and pointed it at the door. Another lawman would die this day. They just kept looking for him. He shot the man as he entered the bar with two bullets. One was just not enough he had found out. He had been wounded once when he shot a man with only one bullet. The man fired at him from a lying position near the door to a bar. He walked over to the man and shot him in the head. Three bullets were better than two. He always used two shots to kill a man now. His shoulder still hurt where that bullet went through his shoulder. Bill was just a killer now.

He reloaded as he walked out of the bar with a swagger. He was Bill the killer. He just went and did what he wanted. He spoke to the bartender.

"The dead guy will pay my tab."

Bill was a killer. It was that simple. He ruled the west because he just killed anyone that wanted him dead. They would pay his bar tabs. Their money was just going to waste if they didn't pay his tab. The bartender gave Bill a thumbs up! He took all the money out of the dead man's wallet. He got a very nice tip.

Bill knew it was time to leave this town. Killing three lawmen meant three lawmen's family's would be looking for revenge. He walked over to his horse, threw his saddlebag over the horse, mounted it and pulled out his pistol. He rode toward the center of town waving his gun over his head and then began shooting it as he rode his horse as fast as it could run. He wanted everyone in town to run for cover, not after him. Bill would need to find another town far from this one. He had worn out his welcome in this town

SADDLEBAG

Now Bill kept everything he felt was valuable in his saddlebag. Every time he had to run from a town was just another time he left everything behind but his saddlebag. Clothes, toiletries, and memories were just things he could find someplace else. In fact he only had bad memories and that was the main reason he became a killer. It was also why he drank so much. He didn't want memories. He tried to have them once when he was a child and that didn't turn out well for him. Now he drank and killed because he didn't want memories. The trouble was that that little child in him still remembered. He took his gun out and reloaded it. He was about to find a new town. He was going to drink and was ready to kill again. That was just the way of the west. He patted his saddlebag. That was all he cared about now. He took his gun out and revolved the chamber. It still clicked like the numbers on a safe. He wasn't sure why he had to do this? It just made him think about drinking and killing.

Bill entered the town by the name of "Peace."

Bill had never heard of it before. He was about to never forget it.

"Peace" was the town Bill never thought he would ever enter. He would now change from a killer into a man. Bill would never shoot his gun again.

"Peace" was a town that Bill has to find. He rode his horse toward a saloon. He stepped off his horse and smiled. He was not thinking like a killer. He was thinking he was just a man.

"Peace" had just taken a hold on him. He drooled. He had become someone he never thought he could become. He dropped his gun. His saddlebag opened. It spilled out a book and a photo. He no longer was a killer. "Peace" now had him by his balls. Bill wasn't himself. He was now a drooling person that needed to find a way to rest in a town that was called "Peace." Bill found a place he needed to find but never thought he could. The book that fell out of his saddlebag opened to page one.

He fell face first down on the dirt that was the town's street.

He drooled and and spit out the words "I am a killer. I don't want to continue killing. Please accept me."

Bill found peace!

It also found him!

A town called "Peace'" was now going to reclaim the most deadly killer the west ever produced.

Bill was now going to find "Peace!"

His gun was no longer a part of him. He just gave it up! He wept before the people in the street that now surrounded him.

|"I am no longer a killer!" He screamed.

Bill wept as he quit his old life.

"I accept "Peace" as my destiny!"

The book that was now opened to page one had a written message from his mother.

"Nothing is worth killing for! Find peace!"

Bill turned into the town drunk in a town named Peace. He would only have drunken memories from now on if he could even remember anything. That was the way of the west! His saddlebag was why he remained a killer and now it was the reason he wasn't one. The photo was a blurred image of him as a child. He had witnessed his parents being shot to death. He killed because it was just the only memory he could remember. The book was his mothers. She only wrote the one line on the final page.

"Find Peace!"

Bill now had found it!

Writer's note:

OK! Most people go into a relationship with a person of interest with some sort of a plan. But what if you found a person of interest that you just couldn't figure out. Drake liked to control everything. Drake met a woman that just didn't fit into any mold that he had ever seen before. Drake tried to control her and she just laughed and got on top while they had sex. Drake tried to talk with her about her feelings and she just told him to make her a cup of coffee. Drake as a man just found out that there is a woman that he would need to take baby steps with. This tale will make men appreciate women. Drake is just a character in this tale. The woman is the main character. She is the one Drake needs to take baby steps with. This little tale will make men think differently about relationships. Cinderella is no fairy tale. It is a tale though. Drake is just a character in this tale that needed to understand what a real woman wants. Read Charlotte's tale!

BABY STEPS

DRAKE IS A VERY SUCCESSFUL lawyer. He is also considered one of the most available bachelors in all of Pennsylvania. He dates the pride of the state's most powerful people's daughters. He is not going to be tricked into a arranged marriage though. His parents keep trying to set him up with the rich and powerful daughters in the state. They even tried to get him interested in the New York debutants. Drake just wants to play the field and not make any commitments. Drake is young, dumb, and not fully aware that females are very different than males. He is about to find out though that they have the most powerful weapon on earth. They want to be equal to their mate. Drake just found out that he was just a man that needed to find a woman his equal which is not easily done in this day and age. He found one though that he could not control. Was she his wake up call? Drake met Charlotte at a beach party. She was dancing by herself in front of a beach fire. She was moving her body to some music that only she could hear. He wanted to hear it also because her body moved so erotically that he wanted some of her. Charlotte motioned with her hand for him to join her. His parents wouldn't approve. He was mesmerized though and joined her. She made him feel the music that was only playing for them. He danced wildly with her to only music the two of them could hear. He became a fool that night. He didn't know it yet, but he had just met the woman that was his equal. He just met the woman he would need to take baby steps with. Drake had met the woman that he could never control. He was now just a passenger on a train that led to he didn't know where. He had just met a woman that he didn't understand and definitely couldn't control.

TOMORROW

Drake met a woman last night that danced to a tune that only he and she could hear. He remembered how she smelled and how she danced. He just didn't remember anything after that. He just woke up in his bed with her next to him and was very confused. Baby steps was all his mind was telling him. Drake was now mesmerized. He asked her what her name was?

She answered, "After you get me coffee."

Drake got up, put on a robe and walked toward the kitchen to get her some coffee. He knew he could use some also. He just didn't understand how he could have lost control? He could only remember dancing with this girl and nothing after that. Now he was bringing her a cup of coffee to just get her name.

SMOOCH

Drake just had the best sex in his life and could't remember having it. He brought his cup and a cup of black coffee to the woman in his bed.

"I don't know how you like it?"

"Hot." was all she said.

He drank his cup as did she. She smiled at him and that made him uncomfortable.

She spoke. "I need to shower. The sex made me sweat."

Drake was so mystified that all he could mutter was, " The bathroom is over there" and pointed.

She stood up naked and he got an erection. She walked effortlessly toward the bathroom. She then turned and motioned for him to follow her.

"Sex in the shower always makes me feel like I am a mermaid."

Drake followed her into the bathroom and then into the shower. He couldn't resist this woman for some reason that didn't follow any of his rules about relationships with women. He would proceed with "baby steps."

CHARLOTTE

Charlotte fucked him two times in the shower and then washed herself in front of him making sure he was watching her do so.

She spoke. "Please watch while I wash away your semen and smell."

She then laughed loud and hard.

"You are a good fuck, but can you satisfy a woman like me?"

Drake was standing wet and naked outside of the shower not knowing what to say or do. He was in unchartered territory with Charlotte. He was a master at controlling a courtroom. Charlotte on the other hand was not so easily seen or manipulated. He was standing naked and unprepared for what he was supposed to do next. He fumbled out the words "I want to try!"

"Then dry off and get dressed for court. You will be defending me against a very powerful and dangerous asshole that wants me erased from this planet. He thinks I am a witch!"

Drake dried himself with a large towel and kept watching the naked Charlotte just watching him do so. She kept licking her lips and throwing him kisses. He was not sure if he was awake or in a dream. Charlotte made him feel like a child waiting for a treat. He was being asked to defend her in court though and that was no treat.

Charlotte just smiled at him as he dressed for court. She had her lawyer and he had had her. She motioned for him to come close to her. She whispered in his ear, "This will not be a cakewalk. This man really wants to convict me as a witch!"

All Drake could think about was "baby steps." Charlotte had her lawyer!

THE COURTROOM

Drake stood up and faced the courtroom. He was just Charlotte's tool now. All he could think about was she did it and why. Now I will have to defend a killer. He stood facing the court. Decision time? "Baby Steps!"

Writer's note:

    What if you were born so white that even your gums were white? I am just saying? The life of a albino is not one you would wish upon anyone. This is a tale that I always wanted to write. I am just not sure it is ready to be told. Welcome to Albino! She needs her story to be told! She is a albino for a reason. Can you accept her story? I writes on!

ALBINO

DOMANO IS SO WHITE THERE needs to be something other than white to describe her. She stares into a mirror and cries. She is so white. Her hair is super blond but it is not a blond that anyone has seen before. She is the albino. She is a freak of nature. She will just have to find a way to exist and her whole life will be Hell. She is worried because she is so different from everyone else. She remembers being called all sorts of names in the schools she attended in the past. She has no friends. Kids are cruel and she was just too different for anyone to want to be close to her. It was easy to make her run from her school to her home in tears. The kids just would chime, She is the white witch that can't cast a spell! "Witchy, Witchy, white as a cloud but can't be one."

Boston was hard on a albino. Domano was born a albino. She was also born in Boston. Witches were perceived as something that just happened there. A albino was so rare that the Boston youth thought of her as one. She was just a frightened little girl though. Even her parents thought she was not normal. She was not even loved by her parents or the other siblings in her family. She lived in the attic of the house her parent's owned. Domano lay down and cried. What was she supposed to do?

Little did she know that every year that she lived made her more powerful in the supernatural world. She would become a white witch, the most rare witch on this planet. Her pillow glowed yellow while she wept on it. She was growing into her powers and didn't even know it. Domano became a full fledged witch on the Halloween of 2016. The White witch of 2016 had just awakened. She now would make Boston Hell! Welcome the "White witch of Boston 2016."

HALLOWEEN 2016

Domano left her house on Halloween of 2016. Her face turned so white that no other color could describe it as a color. She walked down her block and anyone that was on the street ran away. She was glowing with a white fuzzy cloud about her body! Wait, she was emitting a glow that scared any person that looked at her. Domano was now more than just a albino. She was the "White witch of Boston."

Boston was not ready for her, but she was ready for Boston. She walked on as everyone fled from her. She just realized how powerful she had become. Hiding in her parent's attic had made her something Boston had only seen in it's hidden past. She was "The White Witch."

Boston was now going to realize that witches were real. Domano would make them see her as she was now! "The White Witch of Boston."

Legends told of her, but no one alive had ever witnessed one. She was the albino witch that should never have been born.

She now was walking Boston streets as the "White Witch" on Halloween night 2016.

She felt the power of all the witches that were ever burned. Some were witches but the many girls burned who were not witches that were burned haunted her. She still walked on not wanting the locals to forget her walking among them. She was about to give Boston it's wake up call. She was the "White Witch of 2016." "The White Witch" was now more than just a tale told to frighten children. She was walking Boston's streets on Halloween night glowing in a cloud of white light.

THE WHITE WITCH

Domano, now the white witch of Boston just kept walking the streets and felt comfortable. She really didn't want to harm anyone. Everyone ran from her presence. A white witch was very scary to most people. Boston was mostly a alcoholic community. Most people just stared at themselves in a mirror and felt safe in their world. Seeing a white witch was way too much for most of them. Boston needed a white witch to awaken it. Domano just smiled! Boston needed this white witch! Domano continued smiling and headed for down town. There were a lot of bars for her to empty out. She was more than just a person wearing a costume on Halloween of 2016! She was "The White Witch" Boston was not expecting! She was "the Albino turned witch!"

DOMANO

Boston is a large city and it has it's history. Domano entering down town was not something anyone would see unless she was in your presence. She was expelling anyone who saw her coming. All fled the "White Witch of Boston."

Domano was not trying to scare the people of Boston but just wake them up. She had been tortured her whole life because she was a albino. Now she used everything in Boston's history to make her a witch. She was just trying to wake up a city! It needed to awaken!

Domano entered the downtown and walked around it as if it was just a bunch of bricks trying to remember how they became a square where people made decisions. She entered the town square and in front of all Boston's citizens declared that she had become a witch to make Boston understand that life was something more than making a albino girl hate life. She swirled her body and the white fuzz surrounding her covered all who were there. She then spoke loud and clear.

"Wake up! I was never accepted in this world so I took another route. Being a witch will scare most of you and be a blessing for the rest. Boston on this Halloween night of 2016 will become a memory none who are here will ever forget. She then swirled her body so fast that she disappeared.

AFTERMATH

Boston would never be the same again. They realized that they had turned a albino into a witch. Shame on you Boston was all the other cities newspapers could say. They were afraid a witch might call them out! Boston changed what other cities saw witches as. "The White Witch" of Boston in 2016 stirred the brew that most other cities were drinking. It would be their turn next! Domano never really disappeared in a puff of white smoke. She just walked away after making her point to the citizens of Boston. She was heading for New York. She had made her point in Boston. There were other cities that needed her! She would also change her name to "Domino" this time. New York wasn't Boston after all!

Writer's note:

    There are bars everywhere in the cities that dot this planet. Every city, town, parish, and even the little known bayous have them. They all have one thing in common. "The bar stool." This little tale is about that one piece of furniture that is not only necessary but is irreplaceable. I think this tale will scare people into drinking somewhere else than a bar with bar stools. If one is destined for you, then leave the bar. I am just telling a tale of one such bar stool. It could just become the only place that a person could turn to when they have no other place to go!

BAR STOOL

HERCULES ENTERED THE BAR JUST *down the street from his new apartment. He had to downsize and move to a neighborhood he used to avoid. His company demoted him and now he was making a lot less money. He couldn't afford his uptown apartment anymore. In fact he put most of his furniture and accessories in a consignment store. He was trying to figure out what went wrong? He stepped up to the bar and looked around. There were two people sitting at the end of the bar that seemed to be a part of the scenery. He sat down and motioned for the bartender to come over.*

"Three fingers of whatever scotch will not turn my stomach."

Hercules was now part of this new neighborhood. He drank with a very sad face. He didn't like life at this moment. He did find a bar stool that he felt comfortable with though. He ordered another scotch. He was about to find out that this bar was meant for him to find. He had found a bar stool that would change his life forever. Hercules called the bartender over to him.

"I am Hercules."

The bartender responded.

"I am Hank. welcome to Hell's Fountain. It is my bar. Make yourself comfortable."

Hercules moved his ass around the bar stool until he felt comfortable. He looked down the bar to the two other people sitting on their bar stools. He waved at them. They waved back. Hercules just found his bar stool.

"Hell's fountain" just claimed another victim. A bar stool is nothing until it finds it's victim. Hercules just found his! He tried to make himself

comfortable. Hercules just found out that there was a bar stool for him. He rotated it and then spun it to face the bartender.

"I will have a double scotch of your best."

He just then became the owner of a bar stool.

Hank just smiled and said it again "Welcome to Hell's fountain."

Hercules just found out that a bar stool could rule a person's life. He drank his scotch.

HELL'S FOUNTAIN

"Give the guys at the end of the bar a drink on me."

Hercules just became a member of the the bar stools at "Hell's fountain."

Life has so many surprises in it that a person that doesn't find his or her bar stool will never understand that life makes a person look for a bar stool when all else is failing in their life. Hercules just found his bar stool. His past life is now just his past. His new bar stool at "Hell's Fountain" just brought him up to date with who he will become.

"Another double scotch of your best!" was all Hercules could sputter out of his not drunk enough mouth.

Hercules was now at home on a bar stool in a bar he never would have thought he would sit upon a month ago. That is how it is when life sends you a wake up call. Hercules was now owning a bar stool that would control the rest of his life. He opened a door to a bar and found a bar stool that might or may not have been custom fit for him. He for now was just buying drinks for two other bar stools sitting at the opposite end of the bar from him and talking to a bartender by the name of Hank. He felt ok doing so. While drinking his scotch he had a strange thought. What if he was meant to find this bar stool?

HELL'S FOUNTAIN AGAIN

Hank came up to Hercules and asked him if he wanted another?

"WTF. Keep them coming and fill the glasses at the end of the bar."

Hercules could not even remember yesterday. He was spinning in his head. He just found out he belonged in a bar. He found his bar stool. Life to him was now not wanting to remember. He was a successful person living the high life, when all of a sudden the bottom fell out of his world and he was miss casted as the man sitting on a barstool in a saloon by the name of "Hell's Fountain."

Hell was more like it to him. "Hell's Fountain" was just a place he landed in. He did find his barstool though.

Hercules was getting very drunk. He did notice though that the two people sitting at the other end of the bar and he were the only customers in the bar. He motioned Hank over to him.

"When does this place get busy?"

Hank just shrugged his shoulders and walked away saying, "That depends upon how many lost souls need to find a bar stool?"

Hercule's mouth dropped to the bar in front of him. He had found a bar stool and now his future was here. He had no more questions for Hank! He was now at home. A bar stool claimed another victim. He then moved to the end of the bar. His bar stool followed him.

Writer's note:

Why are there people who rule? I think it is because most people need a leader. It is that simple. Most people are so stupid that they would die of starvation without someone supplying them with food. That is why there arc Kings. Sometimes there is a Queen but this is a short tale about a King. I hope this little tale shines a light upon royalty. People need to be ruled. The problem is only a few can do it. The rest are just waiting to be ruled. This kid is not ready, but he is royalty. He will become a king because there is no other choice. He is Royal! He is about to become a King! The rest of his family are in bread and definitely lesser choices. He doesn't want the throne but he will inherit it. He now will become a king! Now a King will tell the world what no King ever spoke of before. He will become a real King because he didn't want to become one but found out how to be one. A very special little tale.

KING

RICHARD WAS BORN INTO A *royal family. He didn't ask to be a royal. He was just supposed to become one. He was looking at his parents and wondered how they kept in charge of their kingdom? He was now 14. He was about to grow into a person that was supposed to lead a kingdom. He was looking for someone to help him grow into a king. He had no clue as how he could become a king. He needed help to find a way. His parents just expected it of him and he could never ask them for help. Royals didn't like to see weakness in their successor. He was being raised by foolish parents and fools that were supposed to be his teachers. Richard knew the history of his family. He had been taught it ever since he could understand the words spoken to him. He had to learn the history of his family in order to take charge of it someday was preached to him every waking hour he lived. He was taught that most royals in his family in the past had wars that allowed them to become leaders. Even his parents had a war. He really didn't want to start a war just to become a king. Even the peaceful royals in his family had become leaders by healing their kingdom after a war. He was puzzled and scared. His parents ruled in a peaceful time. He was supposed to become a leader by what? He needed a guide. He left the castle and went into the woods. He wanted to hunt deer and other animals. He wanted to feel like the supreme predator on this planet. The trouble was he was just a mortal. There was a place in the forest that opened a gate to a world no human could enter was the wive's tale the forest people told to their children. He wanted to be the first king to enter it. He pulled the string on his bow with a arrow that was straight and lethal. He saw a buck disappear into a what he could only* guess at. He ran as fast as he could and entered into the opening the buck disappeared into. He fell to his knees and saw a world that no human before him had ever seen before he guessed. He dropped his bow and arrow and stared at a buck that just stared back at him. He no longer felt like a royal. He felt like a animal that was living in a forest.

The buck spoke to him.

"You are not anything in this world yet!"

Richard stood up not even thinking of picking up his bow and arrow. He spoke to the buck.

"You talk?"

"Yes I do and you no longer are a hunter."

Richard looked at himself and saw himself as just a person. It was something he never thought he would see. He looked at his arms and legs and saw just a being. He was free! He never felt so calm in his life.

He spoke to the buck.

"So, why am I here?"

The buck looked him in his eyes.

"You need to learn that everything in a kingdom has a purpose."

Richard dropped to his knees and sputtered out "I don't know what to do?"

The buck walked around him in a circle.

"You are one pathetic royal and really need some guidance."

Richard rubbed his eyes. He wasn't sure that he was not asleep in his bed just dreaming this.

The buck said "follow me I will show you what you need to become a king."

Richard stood up and followed the buck. He was lost in any world that he could ever imagine. Following a talking deer just might make sense in this world? He knew that he was lost in the other world he just left. Maybe he just might learn something in this one? He was 14 and was expected to rule a kingdom. He needed all the help he could get. He smiled and looked around. He was in world that couldn't exist unless he was to become a king. He shut his eyes and when he opened them he hoped he would be ready to become a king.

Richard was now learning how rule. He just found a talking deer that led him to a place that was going to teach him what a King should be.

RICHARD FINDS HIMSELF

Richard had been led by a talking deer to a world he had to run to find a entrance to. He sucked in his breath and asked the talking deer, "What am I supposed to find in this world?"

The deer just said, "Follow me."

Richard was now so lost that he would only get back to his kingdom and his world if he followed the deer. The deer smiled and said, "follow me."

The deer led him through a series of people making a living by using the land and it's bounties. Richard saw that people were more than just tools. They were tools though but not his. They created his kingdom. He was nothing without them. A Kingdom needed a ruler that respected it's people. The deer led him to the door he entered earlier. He reentered the world he would now rule.

Richard found out becoming a King meant he would need the respect of the people that needed to be ruled. He walked back from the forest to the palace he would inherit. He now knew he could become "King."

Writer's note:

What if you woke up one day and said I will become a serial killer? That is what this little tale is all about. People are strange! A very scary tale. Think about it? I am only writing it because there are some sick mother fuckers out there that need to be destroyed. Read this tale and then never sleep a night without wondering if there is a sick someone out there that might come knocking on your door. Trust me! There are sick mother fuckers out there that want to become this guy I am going to write about him. I am sorry! Life and the press make these individuals real. Whoops! I don't think I want to write this tale.

SERIAL KILLER

MACE AWOKE FROM A DRUNKEN *dream. He at least thought that was what was it was. Mace was weird. He wanted to kill people. He grinned and tried to find a bottle of liquor that wasn't empty. He wanted to be a killer. He was not anything in this world. He wanted to make the news on television. He wanted to become a serial killer. He just took another drink from a bottle of vodka and decided now was the day he would start killing. He had drunk every bottle dry in his one room apartment. He needed to find someone who was willing to sell him a gun. He asked around his neighborhood and finally finds someone who is not so repulsed by him that Mace thinks might help him. The guy tells him that he will sell him a gun and a knife. He will then want him to forget he ever met him. He doesn't like Mace. In fact he is afraid of him. I mean he is really frightened by Mace. He charged him double what he would charge anyone else for the weapons though. He just made sure the knife was sheathed and the gun was not loaded. He ran away with the money and didn't ever want to look back.*

Mace is ready to begin killing and he won't stop until he makes it on the morning television news. He thinks he is going to be a serial killer if he just can get past his first kill. He goes back to his apartment and tries to decide how he will kill his first victim? He is sick and tired of being a nobody. He wants to be on the morning news and on all the news shows on television at night. He wants to become a serial killer. He just has to plan it out. Mace decides to write a diary. He goes to Staples and buys a diary book. He writes on the cover of the diary, "A serial killer's story." Mace is insane.

Writer's note: This tale is not for beginners. Please pass it by if you are afraid that you may want to become Mace. He is not a tale I want to see ever happen.

MACE

Mace is working at a Safeway store as a stocker. That means lousy hours and very boring work. He fills the shelves with crap that most people buy. Mostly crap as far as he is concerned. He has been on the job for four years and he mostly fills the shelves with junk food. He is sick of the every day shopper. They just buy crap. He just keeps the shelves full. He woke up this morning with just a little smile on his face. He bought a gun and got a knife as a bonus. He now wants to become his dream. He wants to become a serial killer. He has studied them. He has been to many libraries in his city and and has read about the most famous ones. He wants to be more famous than any of them. The problem is he doesn't know how to begin his killings. He can't be the best unless he kills better than anyone else that he has read about. He rubs his eyes and leans back in his recliner. He is now going to become the best serial killer that has ever been. He just needs to make his first kill special. He reclines his recliner and starts to freak out. He needs to become a killer. Mace is now going to change from what he was into a killer. He throws a fit. He is not in control of his body. It is moving in ways no body should. He calms down. He stands up and goes to where he hides his gun and knife. He holds the gun in one hand and the knife in the other. He will use them both on each kill. No one has ever killed with both a gun and a knife the way he imagines doing it that he has read about. He will set the world on fire with killings using both in a way only he could think up He is going to rewrite serial killing. He will kill with a knife and kill again with a gun. He will kill two people each time he kills. He smiles. He will rewrite the serial killer. He goes back to his recliner and sits down and reclines it. He is going to kill. He is just not sure how to start his killings. He falls asleep in his recliner.

MACE BEGINS HIS KILLING SPREE

Mace awakes to the morning news. He fell asleep without turning off his television. He is late for work. He picks up his cell phone and dials his boss. He tells him he has a flu and his doctor wants him to take a week off to recuperate. He will not be coming to work this week. He will be starting his new job as a serial killer. He just needs to find his first victims. He will spend the rest of the day reclining in his recliner trying to figure out just who could possibly be the first victims in a series that he will perform as the serial killer he wants to become. No one will see him coming! He holds the gun above his head and kisses the knife in his left hand. He switches hands. The knife is now in his right hand. The gun is now in his left hand. He will kill each of his victims with both hands and now he wants to master using his weapons with either hand. He practices while watching the news on his television. He imagines himself as the lead story each and every morning. He is truly insane and that makes him the perfect person to become a serial killer.

SCOUTING FOR VICTIMS

Mace has lived a solitary life. Killing two people at once makes him very nervous. His neighbors have never talked to him and he has lived in his apartment for four years. He watches the morning news without really hearing it. He is lost in his fucked up mind set of being the best serial killer ever. He goes to his hiding places and takes out his knife and gun again. He holds them to his chest and speaks out loud to no one in particular except himself.

"I am going to become the most feared serial killer that has ever lived."

He puts the weapons back in their hiding places. He really doesn't understand why he has to hide them. They are just as lethal out in the open. He smiles and walks toward the door to his apartment. He leaves with a crooked smile on his face. He needs to find his prey. He walks away from his apartment intent on finding his first two victims. He goes to a busy park and sits on a bench that would give him a good view of who was coming and going from the park. Victims were not so easily discovered in his first five hours. Daytime seemed the wrong time for him to find victims. He walks awhile and then buys a hot dog and a drink from a vendor and takes another seat on one of the benches. He has a long day ahead of him.

VICTIMS ONE AND TWO

Mace eats his hot dog and drinks his drink. He studies the people that come to the park when the sun is setting. He sees a new breed, or as he sees it, a new pool of victims. He smiles his crooked smile and rubs his head. He now knows that he will kill when the sun sets. He watches the people looking for a couple or maybe just two people that are not aware he is watching them. He rubs his hand over his gun and the other hand on the knife's handle. He is ready. The problem is he has no victims picked out. He walks back to his apartment frustrated. He sits in his recliner waving the gun and knife between both hands. He must get this right is all he can think about. He will wait until sunset tomorrow before he looks for victims. He just keeps moving the gun and knife between both hands. He wants his first kill to be the one that makes his signature. Both of his hands want blood. He keeps changing hands with his weapons. He will not sleep until he kills his first two victims. He goes to the park again and watches everyone. He needs to find two victims that will make his desire to kill be fulfilled. He is patient. He needs two people to kill.

A woman is stretching her legs on a park bench. A man comes up to her and asks her something. They seem to be perfect for his first kill. He moves quickly toward them pulling out his pistol and the knife. He tries to shoot the man but he side stepped the shot. The woman starts running. The man pulls out a gun from behind his back and shoots Mace in the face. He is a policeman out for a run. He always keeps a gun handy. He looks down at Mace's dead face and wonders what he was thinking. Mace was not really a serial killer. He just wanted to be one. The officer who shot him in the face just wondered why a man would try to attack two people in a park. Mace would never be known as a would be serial killer. He was just a dead man in a park. So much for his wanting to be famous. He was just a perp that got shot in a park. Mace was just another story that never got written. Thank goodness!

Writer's note.

A girl was born with bright green eyes. She is very rare. She is the emerald among the rest of the jewels that exist. When she was born her parents named her Emerald Holly Perkins. They had never seen a child with green eyes like this before. She was special to them and they named her after a gem. She used Holly as her name while she was growing up. Emerald was just too strange of a name for a kid. Holly grew up though knowing her first name was Emerald. She also knew she had special green eyes. She knew that she was that rare a gem. This is her tale.

GREEN EYES

HOLLY WAS A BANK TELLER *at First Houston Credit Union. It paid more than what banks paid most of their tellers, but it was still not a lot of money coming in each month. She was gorgeous, not just beautiful. Her green eyes sparkled at night and her red hair was like no other redhead before her. She turned into Emerald when the sun set. She prowled the bars of Houston looking for rich drunks. None of them could resist her. She made ten times her credit union salary in a day. Rich men in Houston were as stupid as they looked. She usually chose married men and took as much from them as she felt she could before discarding them. They only knew her as Emerald. She made sure that they wouldn't talk by taking videos of the love making, or whatever you called it, on her cell phone that she positioned before the sex. She always turned the phone over to the mark after her final payday. They were untraceable phones. She was just Emerald. She floated from bar to bar and just chose the most vulnerable rich dicks. Houston was filled with them. They drank too much and had too much to lose if she told on them. They all were just stupid good old boys that never grew up. After Emerald they were at least 6 inches shorter. Emerald was just Holly during the daytime hours, but at nightfall, beware all you good old boys! Emerald was a bitch that you good old boys needed to avoid!*

EMERALD'S DAYTIME JOB

Holly was the opposite of Emerald. She wore colored lens so she looked blue eyed and wore glasses with just plain lenses. She wore very unrevealing dresses and covered up most of her body. She pulled her hair back and made it a bun. She was just the gal everyone would want to take home to their mothers. The marks were just customers to her when the sun set though. She was a shark among unprotected fools that had money. She just took enough and then forgot them. They or she would never see each other again. At least that is what she thought. Even a city as large as Houston had some private dicks that were not so stoned or stupid as to be able to figured out there was a "Emerald" out there and money could buy them just as easily as Emerald could take it away from the marks.

Enter "Charlie Bloodhound Perkins."

CHARLIE "BLOODHOUND" PERKINS

Now Leonard Wilson was not very happy to be taken by a whore. He had the phone that this Emerald had given him after fleecing him for close to twenty grand. He hired a private eye by the name of Charlie "Bloodhound" Perkins to find Emerald and expose her to the world. He was being divorced anyways and a scandal was now not going to hurt his alimony payments. He just felt that Emerald had taken money that his soon to be ex wife would have gotten anyways. He just was a good old boy that wanted to stay one. Charlie "Bloodhound" Perkins was the best in the business at finding people. Leonard turned the phone over to Charlie and gave him twenty five hundred dollars with a promise of fifty thousand more if he could find this Emerald and bring her to one of his ranches.

This was all Charlie needed to get him sniffing around. Houston was a cesspool, but a rare gem like Emerald would soon glow bright somewhere. Charlie was on the job! Charlie didn't get his nickname because he wasn't what he promised, "a bloodhound."

He took the phone to a friend who might get some fingerprints of this "Emerald.

HOLLY

Now Charlie was no fool and Holly wasn't either. She wiped all the phones she gave her marks with a kleenex with a lotion for making the kleenex a skin softener. It got rid of fingerprints and left a greasy film on the cameras. Whoever touched it next would leave theirs. Charlie just got Leonard's fingerprints off the camera. He smiled. This "Emerald " would be a challenge for him.

Holly was happy today. She was having her 21st birthday. She was given a birthday party by her fellow workers at the credit union. She blew out the candles and went back to work after eating a piece of the cake. She was after all Holly. Tonight though she would again be "Emerald" and her turning 21 was going to make one stupid good old boy in Houston pay! Holly smiled as she passed the daytime hours away. Tonight she would sparkle as "Emerald" turning 21. She wanted to make this night special. She would prowl the bars of Houston in hopes of finding a special mark. She wanted to make her twenty first birthday to be special and some rich dick out there was about to pay handsomely.

CHARLIE "BLOODHOUND PERKINS"

Holly, now Emerald was wary! She felt uncomfortable hunting tonight. The rich dicks she was targeting now had a hunter looking for her and she felt his presence. She always knew it would happen someday. Turning twenty one just made her into a woman that had a past. She was now wondering how to make a future in Texas?

She would have to erase Holly and become "Emerald."

Let the past catch up to who she really was!

Enter Holly

Holly was scared. she knew Emerald was not going to enter this night. You could not forget what never happened. Emerald was a person Holly never thought she would become. Holly just turned 21. She now would leave "Emerald" behind.

"Happy Birthday" Holly! She left Houston and the "bloodhound" behind her. Welcome Chicago!

Writer's note:

Many bands want the spotlight. Only a few get it. What if you had a midget that had the answer to making you famous? He was not dressed well and stank very bad. He just told the band who was on break from a bad set and that they were going to make it big if they just cleaned him up. The drummer walked over and hugged him.

"Lead us on little toad!"

That became his name and the bands. "Little Toad."

The band took him to a hotel and bathed and shaved him. They then changed their name to "Little Toad." They were now on the road to success. What they didn't know was that "Little Toad" was not who he claimed to be. They would find out the road to success barely ever began by picking up a hitch hiker. Especially one by the name "Little Toad." Quite a tale!

ROCK AND ROLL HELL

"LITTLE TOAD" WAS NOW ON *tour. They had a midget or as he liked to be called "Little Toad" as their lead singer. His voice was pretty much like a toad's voice, or at least what most people expected a toad to sound like. He was very repulsive and the press just loved that part about him. They were a success at every stage they played upon. "Little Toad" was a band that everyone wanted to see play their strange music.*

But the band "Little Toad" was about to meet the real midget, or as he liked to call himself, "The Dwarf king."

The Dwarf King

Little Toad was on tour. They were strange but people liked the fact that they were led by a midget. The problem was the midget. He was not what you call human.

He really was more like a toad! He just couldn't become a human. The band though, was so successful that no one really saw what "Little Toad" did away from the stage. The rest of the band members avoided him at every chance meeting. They needed him but wanted nothing to do with him. There wasn't a groupie that ever met him that wanted anything to do with him. The band just left him alone. They just hired a guy to make sure he showed up for the performances. All went well for a year. Then "Little Toad" decided to show the audience who he really was.

THE FINAL PERFORMANCE

"Little Toad" was due on stage in New Orleans. The midget or "Little Toad" as he liked to be called smiled before going on stage. His band was snorting all sorts of drugs. They could afford any and all that was available. The midget or "Little Toad" just smiled as he took the microphone.

"I don't do drugs! I don't fuck the groupies. In fact I am the most boring super star that ever took a stage. I am a Dwarf. Now I guess you are asking yourselves what is a dwarf? Tolkien made them a species in his books. We were here long before him. We were miners. We fit into places humans couldn't."

He then paraded around the stage showing just how small he was. He admitted that he ate bugs. He had a tongue that could protrude about three feet and he ate bugs! He was "The Dwarf King."

The audience hushed so loud that even a moth's wings would make more noise.

The Dwarf King just kept moving around in a circle on the stage. He wanted the audience to see him as he truly was. "The Dwarf King."

He walked to the center of the stage and stared out at the crowd that came to see a music performance.

"I am not a freak of nature. I am nature just letting you fools know we are not just something a writer created. We are just deciding to show ourselves to you."

The crowd was getting restless. They wanted to see a band not a midget telling them that he was a Dwarf king. They started throwing things at the dwarf.

He just turned his back and let the litter fly at him.

He then turned and faced the crowd. He spoke loud so everyone could hear him.

"I am just "Little Toad" to you. I am the door opening to what will soon make this world look at the supernatural as an everyday adventure."

He then walked off stage and farted with each step he took.

AFTERMATH

"*Little Toad*" *or whoever he was just disappeared after he left the stage. The band was nothing without him and the audience started throwing anything they could get their hands on at the band. The band ran for cover. "Little Toad" went back to being a smelly midget living near trash and garbage containers. He made the world see a "Dwarf King!" Now they would possibly see some more supernatural creatures. He opened the door by appearing on stage. He smiled as he jumped into a container that was outside a restaurant. They always had the best garbage. The world was not ready for his kind. He just would fill his belly with garbage. The world would just have to wait for the next act a supernatural being would decide to walk on a stage and create. Garbage right now was all "Little Toad" needed. He shot his tongue out and caught a fly.*

"*Yes the world was not ready for the supernatural or the dwarf king.*"

Writer's note:

What if you woke up one morning with puss oozing sours covering your body. How would you react? I guess you wouldn't want to look into a mirror. Your world and everybody else's would just change. You have the plague. It is not something you were expecting. Welcome this nightmare into your future life. There is no cure for this plague. You just have to live with it. I am not going to tell you this tale has a happy ending. The plague is just the worst nightmare you ever could awake up to. My character just decides to enjoy one day at a time. He just found out that he has no other choice but to not give a shit. You live or die with "The Plague." Read on.

THE PLAGUE

JOHN WOKE UP SWEATING, COUGHING, *and almost blind. He was fine the night before when he and some friends were drinking at a bar and shooting pool. Today was different though. He could barely stand up. He shuffled toward his bathroom sink and tried to focus his eyes on his image in the mirror. What he could barely make out was a horror story. He had sores all over his body and his eyes were almost swollen shut. He couldn't even think that this was just a dream. He was sick. He puked up some nasty flem that he even didn't want to look at. He crawled toward his sofa. He wanted to sleep. He just barely got his body on the sofa. He reached for the blanket he kept on it. He also had a pillow there. He was sweating so bad that he even wasn't sure he could sleep.*

He dry heaved with his head facing the floor. He just thought maybe if he slept he would wake up from this nightmare. He had the plague though. He would wake up, but he would still be oozing puss from sores on his body. He was just going to pass out from his body giving in to the sickness it had found. He went to blank. I mean he just passed out because it was the only way he could live. What he would wake up to was not a question, but a decision. Could he continue to live with the plague? Only tomorrow would answer his question. He just hoped he had one.

TOMORROW

John opened his eyes. He was lying on his living room floor. He had crawled toward his bathroom. He was weak but had enough energy to crawl. He finally made it to his bathroom but didn't know if he could stand up. He reached up to the bowel. The bowel was in his grasp and he finally pulled himself up to a standing position of some sort. He looked at his body and saw a nightmare that even he could never imagine in a thousand years. His body was nothing but puss dripping sores. He tried to scream but even his insides were full of puss. He let himself fall to the floor and gurgled out some of the puss clogging his breathing. He wasn't sure what his body would do next. It was secreting puss from his anus, ears, mouth and everywhere else. He only knew that he was not brain dead yet. He lay oozing puss from anywhere it could ooze. He lay on a cool floor though. That was all his mind could give him.

John puked again but this time it wasn't putrid. He sucked in his breath and somehow felt like he was breathing again. John wasn't ready to give up. He raised himself again and looked into a mirror that showed him a ghost of what he used to be. He choked out a lot of flem that had many colors. He wasn't sure whether he was going to make it to another sunrise. He fell on the cold tile floor of the bathroom. He lost his consciousness.

TOMORROW AGAIN

John awoke to a tiled bathroom floor covered in puss and maybe vomit. He wasn't quite sure. He lifted himself by reaching the sink and pulling himself to a standing position. He saw a pitiful skeleton of a man in the mirror. He was just glad his eyes could still see something. A nightmare would be a welcome site right now. John just threw up and pissed in his underwear. He fell on the cold tile floor of his bathroom. He crawled toward the toilet. He hoped that he could just pull himself up enough to puke into something other than the floor. John was not ready to die. The problem was that he was puking and oozing puss from all parts of his body that could leak. He really had to think that death would be better than what he was living with. "The Plague!" It was real! John died trying go find a toilet. A short tale like this is a blessing!

"The plague."

Writers note:

What if two men met on an island and just talked to each other as men? What if one was young and wanted to become somebody and the other was older and already had made a mark on this world. The older one did so again on the island. He made people wealthy. The younger man asked how he did it? The older man just said, "Never show fear."

The younger man didn't understand the older man's wisdom. He was afraid.

The older man sat at his table on his lanai drinking coffee with the younger man and spoke candidly.

"Don't fear tomorrow. Accept it as the next step toward the beginning. There is no end, just endless beginnings."

This tale is not for the timid. Trust the older man's wisdom. He has had many beginnings. The younger man became his apprentice this day. Read this tale and wonder if you will ever meet this older man? I hope so. He is no stranger when it comes to beginnings. He just might make you one of his apprentices. This tale deals with the supernatural. Get ready to find a new beginning each day in your life. Beginnings lead to an end though. Once you meet the old man you have to become someone. You can never be who you were. You will have to find a new ending to your life. This tale just might not have one though! Tales are at the end of a body! I wag this one on!

NOBODY SAW HIM COMING

RUSSELL WAS AN ISLAND BOY. *He lived on the Big Island of Hawaii his whole life. He met a mainlander that came to the islands. He was not like any other hoale he had ever met. Most were washouts or losers. This guy was just taking a break. The man just didn't fit into the hoale mode that was coming to the island. He was confident, self centered, and so full of himself that he scared the island people. He seemed to not give a shit if he pissed people off. He just wanted to find a place to vegetate. The Big Island though was small and the natives wanted to know who he was. He just didn't give a shit! He just came to the islands to relax and recharge his batteries. Russell met him one day on his lanai drinking Kona coffee. The older man spoke to Russell like he was a man.*

"What are you looking for?"

Russell had never been asked this question. He was just an island boy that was not sure of anything. He stuttered. "I am not sure."

"Then you need to find something to look for."

Russell looked down at his feet. They were useless to him at this moment. "Where do I look?"

"Where you want to go" was the older man's response.

Russell just started shaking. He never thought about a future before. He now saw himself looking for a answer. The older man just kept drinking his coffee. Russell looked at the older man and changed into a new person. He was now the older man's apprentice. He became a new man.

The older man from the mainland had something he needed. Russell just became a new man when in his presence. The older man said he had to move on. *Russell just smiled. He had met a prophet, or at least he thought so. The older man had burned his bridges on the big island and then packed his belongings to go back to the mainland leaving Russell to fend for himself. The older man gave him parting gifts and left the big island forever. He had what he came for. He was recharged. Russell now had to become the older man and find a apprentice. The older man gave Hawaii a leader. Russell went on to become a person that created many new businesses on the big island but never found someone he could teach the way the older man taught him. He missed him and wanted to find him again. The trouble was that the older man from the mainland was constantly moving on to places he needed to find. Russell was just his apprentice. He could never be the older man. Someone somewhere was sitting on a deck drinking coffee with the older man. He just made apprentices. They just couldn't become him. They were just his shadows! The older man is smiling on a deck somewhere. His apprentices are trying to become him. He just smiles and drinks the best coffee the place he is sitting at has to offer. He will move on tomorrow. There is another patio, lanai, or balcony that he has to teach some child to become someone special in this world. The older man is just a teacher. He is never the one that has to learn. He is a teacher. Just beware of a older man sitting on a patio or whatever drinking coffee. He may just change your life. If you meet him don't become his apprentice. He is only the teacher. His apprentices are just going to wander through life making the world a better place. They also will never forget that they were taught to become something in this world. The old man just was their ticket out of a useless life. Some of them feel blessed and some of them feel cursed. They all were made special by a old man drinking coffee on a balcony somewhere. He is still drinking coffee and teaching apprentices on this planet. He is always moving trying to teach the next generation. He is what we call life. Beware if you drink coffee with him. You just might have to make something of your life.*

Writers note:

What if you were just a guy that woke up to a nightmare? You were working at a bar as a bouncer one day and the next you were a slave? What the Hell happened in one night that could do this to you? Yeah! A wake up call in mega proportions. I am just saying this tale is more than cool. It is mega cool. Read on my friends. This could have become a novel?

THE SLAVE

Rufus had just come back to Texas from his second war. He had paid his dues and now had little or no money to show why he fought those wars. He was a bouncer at a Galveston, Texas bar and had to hire on as a fisherman most months to pay his rent and food bills. He wasn't damaged by the wars he fought, at least not physically. He just was a big tough looking guy that most people just minded their own business around because they knew he was capable of really doing bodily harm to them if they didn't. He worked the week days as a bouncer and hired himself out on shrimp boats on weekends. He was just glad that he came home from the wars he fought. Many of his buddies didn't and some of those that did make it back were really damaged goods. Rufus was sitting in a yard in a plastic patio chair next to the apartment complex he was living in drinking a Lone Star long neck and staring at the oil drum fire raging sparks into the cool Texas night. He and some others gathered driftwood from the beach near them and it made a nice fire to sit around and watch the stars. He wasn't alone. There were most of the people that lived in his apartment complex sprawled around the oil drum only moving when they had to throw another piece of driftwood on the fire or go get another Lone Star. Rufus burped loud and heard it echo into the night. No one sitting around the drum fire cared that he disturbed the silence of a Texas night on a beach. In fact a few more burps and farts were heard. These people were just happy to have a oil drum fire and a plastic beach chair to be sitting in while listening to the waves break on the beach and look up at stars in the sky. That was about to end though. This was the night the "Conquerors" landed.

THE CONQUERORS

The aliens landed and started taking humans as slaves. They made them strip and washed them and then gave them uniforms. They were just animals to the aliens. One of the captives was a soldier though and he didn't want to become a slave to a race that conquered a planet and used it's inhabitants as slaves. He was now a slave though. He just didn't become a pacifist one. He was just looking at "The Conquerors" as the enemy. He was a soldier and he would die before giving in to a foe! He bit his tongue and was fed food that tasted like the slop you would feed pigs in Texas. These aliens were not invincible because he had seen two wars and knew all foes had weaknesses. He was just looking for their weakness. He just might have found it. They didn't think that anyone would fight back. Were they ever wrong! Rufus was not going to become a slave. He was their weakness. He just needed to find other soldiers.

Rufus

Rufus was being washed by aliens and he was not enjoying it. He stood and took the hosing because he didn't know how it happened. He was sitting on a beach drinking a lone star looking at the stars and then they landed and took everyone prisoner. It happened so fast that he couldn't even fight back. He was being hosed by creatures that looked to be somewhat humanlike, but more alien than human. He guessed that they had made studies of humans before they landed and took control. The enemy always thought that they were superior, but more times than not they were just prisoners themselves. He was sure these invaders were just soldiers following orders. He was counting on it. He would now just let them take him to the place he would find his army. Creatures that try to make slaves of people always leave openings for an uprising. Rufus would just make sure when it happened he would not be dead.

THE UPRISING

Rufus was a soldier. He had survived when most men he knew didn't. He didn't really find being taken prisoner by aliens as something he could accept. He wanted to understand the creatures that thought they could conquer a planet. He wished he was sitting in that beach chair staring at the stars and drinking a Lone Star Beer. He had been hosed off and sent to someplace that he really didn't think he would enjoy. He didn't miss a thing. The aliens were just like any soldiers he had ever met. They would show him their weakness eventually. Soldiers like Rufus never sleep when they needed to find an answer to how to escape. He just needed a army! He was trying to find some other soldiers. He was in luck. The aliens took a military base as hostages. Rufus had his army. Aliens that thought they were in control just didn't see Rufus coming. He fell down and pretended to be hurt. He would go to the hospital to recruit. He was on a mission. Aliens can not win was all he was thinking! He had to get to the military base that was conquered when he and his apartment dwellers were. He would lead his fellow humans on an uprising.

RUFUS AGAIN

The aliens shot him in the head with a weapon he would never understand. They were Conquerors. He died before the conquest.

Authors that inspired me are few and far between. I will give you some names in no special order. Jules Verne, Aldous Huxley, Rod Serling, Larry McMurtry, Papa Hemingway, Edgar Allen Poe, Gene Roddenberry, Mario Puzo, Mark Twain and of course Tolkien. OK, Stephen King will get a mention. Many more kept me reading and I thank them for being able to mold my mind into a writer. We need to be inspired by the written word and the imagination that it takes to create characters and new worlds to explore. I bow down in front of my fellow writers. May we write on and may someone read us and try to become the next writer.

Printed in the United States
By Bookmasters